The Lady's Reckless Abandon

SAFELY IN SCOTLAND, BOOK 1

ALLISON B. HANSON

ARE YOU SIGNED UP FOR DRAGONBLADE'S BLOG?

You'll get the latest news and information on exclusive giveaways, exclusive excerpts, coming releases, sales, free books, cover reveals and more.

Check out our complete list of authors, too!

No spam, no junk. That's a promise!

Sign Up Here

www.dragonbladepublishing.com

Dearest Reader;

Thank you for your support of a small press. At Dragonblade Publishing, we strive to bring you the highest quality Historical Romance from some of the best authors in the business. Without your support, there is no 'us', so we sincerely hope you adore these stories and find some new favorite authors along the way.

Happy Reading!

CEO, Dragonblade Publishing

Dedication

In memory of Julie Hinkle Smith.
The flowers are for you, my friend.

Chapter One

May 1812

SUNLIGHT STREAMED THROUGH the dingy curtains of the inn as Lady Lily Cantrell stretched and smiled. It would be a lovely day for a wedding. Even if it was to be a hasty affair as soon as they arrived in Scotland, it would be the happiest event of her life. For she was marrying for love.

Turning to look at the empty bed and rumpled sheets, she felt her cheeks warm with memories of the night before. She and her betrothed had anticipated their vows, but it was only by one day.

Not even a full day really, as they planned to wed as soon as they got over the border later that morning. What difference could a single day make?

She couldn't wait to marry Reggie. By this evening, she would be Mrs. Reginald Flockton, and no one would ever know of their minor indiscretion the night prior. It would be something they would laugh about for the rest of their lives together.

Sighing, she threw back the covers and frowned at the evidence of her virtue on the sheet. She'd always thought she would give this gift to her husband on their wedding night, but Reggie had convinced her it would be better to get through that part last night. So their wedding night would be free of discomfort or any untidiness. She had agreed, not just because she was near to dizzy from his kisses, but because she had been worrying over it so. She decided it would be better to get past such anxieties as quickly as possible.

She would never tell another soul, but she did find the act quite unremarkable and exceedingly quick. She wondered why others thought it to be so grand. And by *others* she referred to her twin, Maxwell, and her younger brother by less than a year, Matthew, who both spoke on the topic incessantly.

Perhaps it would be different after she was married. Another grin bloomed when she realized she would know the answer to that question soon enough.

Besides…if she didn't particularly care for it, she would surely not be expected to do it *every* night.

She would deal with that later. As she brushed her hair, she saw her smile reflected back to her in the looking glass. She had never seen herself look so happy before. Today would be perfect. She and Reggie would travel the last few hours into Scotland and be married straight away.

Yes, it would have been lovely if she'd been able to marry in a church, as her three older sisters had, with her family in attendance. But her father, the Marquess of Devon, would never allow one of his daughters to marry the third son of a baron. Even if it was the daughter he hardly even noticed. But at two and twenty, Lily had well reached her majority and could marry without her father's permission.

If it would've made any difference to share with the man how in love she and Reggie were, she might have tried, but Reggie was sure her father wouldn't be convinced. So, instead they had chosen to elope.

It was surely the most scandalous thing she'd ever done, but no one would care after she returned to Town as a married woman. Her father might fuss a bit and her mother would likely swoon, but after the shock they would just be pleased not to have a spinster daughter under their roof any longer.

Donning her robe, Lily went to the door and requested a maid to help her dress for her special day. She imagined Reggie waiting for her downstairs, and the way his face would light up when she joined him for breakfast in her new gown.

After washing the soreness away from her wicked activities, Lily had the maid help her into her finest dress. The woman even did her hair with some fancy curls and a few fresh flowers.

"We only had the primroses blooming in the garden this early in May, miss."

"They are lovely," Lily said with a smile that seemed as if it might never go away. She went to her reticule to offer the woman a coin for her efforts and was surprised to find it empty.

"My apologies, Abby, I will have to get your coin from my fiancé who is waiting downstairs."

The woman smiled, and with a quick dip turned to leave the room.

Lily stopped her to ask, "Do you know how far it is to Scotland from here?"

She hoped they would not have so long to wait. It seemed everything had been a whirlwind since he'd taken an interest in her just two weeks ago. Soon enough they would be wed and things could slow down.

The woman blinked at Lily and shook her head.

"Pardon miss, but you're already in Scotland."

"We are?" Lily laughed. Reggie had been mistaken when he'd said they would have to stop for the night and finish their journey the next day. How amusing he would find it to know they could have married last night after all.

Unless he'd planned it as a surprise. If so, she would play along so not to ruin it.

Reggie's things had already been packed and taken downstairs. Lily's heart warmed knowing her husband-to-be was eager to be on their way so he could marry her.

She knew her family would not be happy when she returned to London a married woman, but it wasn't as if she had done much else to please them. She was the fourth daughter, which would have been enough reason for her to go unnoticed, but having been born mere minutes after the heir had put her firmly in the shadows.

The only time anyone in her family ever took notice of her was when she did something wrong. And while eloping might seem to be another of those things, and they would think she was reckless, it wouldn't matter what they thought any longer, for she would be married and would no longer need to worry about disappointing them.

Her marriage would not only bring her happiness and love, it would bring freedom from her family's reproach. She would no longer be forgotten or overlooked, for Reggie loved her. She didn't think anyone ever would.

Lily gathered her small portmanteau that held her other dress and went down to see her impatient groom.

When she didn't find him waiting in the public room, she chuckled, thinking how romantic he was to have splurged on a private dining room for them that morning. But that room was empty as well.

She stepped outside the tavern, thinking perhaps he'd already ordered their carriage to be brought around so they could make haste, but there was no one out front.

Going back inside, she stopped the innkeeper.

"Pardon, did you see my husband this morning?" She had thought Reggie quite worldly to think to tell the innkeeper they were already a married couple so they might share a room.

The innkeeper looked rather surprised as he looked toward the front door, and then back to her.

"I'm sorry, my lady, but the man left hours ago."

"Hours ago?" She shook her head.

"Aye."

"Perhaps you've confused my husband with someone else. I'm looking for the lanky man, just a bit taller than I am with the charming smile."

"Don't know about a charming smile, but I recall the scrawny fellow who looked a bit like a ferret that came here with ye last night. That's the gent who left here just after dawn." The man went on about his duties as if he had not just blown her over like a feather.

The man described Reggie fairly accurately—while she didn't appreciate her betrothed being likened to a ferret, to some it might seem a proper comparison—so she didn't think he had made a mistake. But that would mean…

"Oh, dear." At first the very idea that Reggie might have intentionally left her behind seemed laughable, but as she looked around the establishment again only to find the man who had rushed her out of London to marry her was still not inside, a sound between a laugh and a groan erupted from her throat.

Lily had never swooned in her life, but as the tavern began to whirl around her, and the facts began to align, she decided if she were ever going to faint, now would be the perfect time.

Chapter Two

FINNEAS LOCKHART, DUKE of Granton, frowned as he parted the curtain in his traveling coach to see the sun was moving closer to the horizon. With only two hours left before arriving home to *Gealach* Castle, they would need to stop for a meal and fresh horses.

He had hoped to keep going so he could finally be home. It had been near to sweltering in London for only being May, and he'd wanted to abandon the heat.

Frowning again, he knew the weather wasn't the only reason he'd wished to leave town.

His dear friends, Shay and Reese, understood why Finn hadn't been enjoying the Season to its fullest this year. But it seemed the rest of the ton, didn't know nor care.

Running his hand over his sleeve, he was still surprised not to encounter the black band there indicating he was in mourning. Technically he had been out of mourning for his dear sister in February, but unfortunately the end of a mourning period did not bring about the end of missing someone.

"I know what you would say, dear sister. That I'm a goose for being so forlorn with your loss all these months later. But you know what I would say to that."

As children, Finn used the excuse of him being the heir to the dukedom as the reason everything should go in his favor. Juniper, however, was rarely ever in agreement. He smiled at the memory, and rapped on the roof of the coach to tell the driver they should stop at the next tavern.

In truth, while he was ready for his journey to end, and he was eager to quit London, he wasn't truly looking forward to being at *Gealach* alone either. It seemed he couldn't find a place to be at peace.

He remembered the castle being a place full of laughter when his parents and sister had lived there with him. But one by one he'd lost his family.

His mother and infant brother had died days apart. The old duke had done his best to be there for Finn and Juniper, but Finn could tell their father was never the same and would often find him sitting in his study with a glass of whisky doing nothing but looking out the window at his wife's garden.

But even with less smiles and laughter from his father, he and June had daily adventures filled with fun and happiness.

Then their father had taken ill when Finn was only ten and six. And while he'd not been prepared to become the duke while attending Heriot's School in Edinburgh, it was thrust upon him nonetheless.

He'd left and come home to stay with June, finishing his schooling with private tutors and keeping up with his friends through correspondence. For more than ten years he and June had lived together in the large castle on the hill.

He made his way to London for the Season each year, and each year he begged June to come with him, but she had refused.

And then last year while he'd been visiting Reese, she'd taken ill. He'd barely made it home in time to say his goodbyes.

Despite all that June could not do for herself in her last days, she had never made Finn feel as he often felt with other people. As if he was needed for something. It seemed everyone needed *The Duke*. Whether it be to invest in something, or to vote a certain way. No one just wanted… Finn.

He loved his friends but even they often looked at him as a peer rather than just a man.

And the young women scouring the ballrooms for a husband, didn't care who he was as a person so long as he was titled and rich.

June had never cared about any of that. To her he was simply a brother.

If ever he decided to marry, he would choose a bride who wanted him, rather than needed him.

The coach slowed and Finn brushed the dust from his coat in preparation for when it stopped and he was free to exit. He looked forward to stretching his long legs. While his coach was built for a man of his size, it was still uncomfortable to be sitting for hours on end. Especially for someone who had grown so restless these last months.

When the door was opened, he practically sprung from his seat. He spoke with the coachman about the arrangements and when he would be ready to depart before turning to enter The Old Forge tavern.

As he moved to the three wide steps that led to the door of the establishment, he noticed a woman sitting on the middle step. At first, he assumed her to be a doxy waiting for a customer to happen by, but then he took in the detail of her gown, and realized she was a proper lady. Despite the redness of too much sun on her face and arms, and the wilted flowers in her limp coiffure.

Keeping to his own business, he nodded in her direction before passing, though it didn't look as if she'd noticed him at all as she stared blankly down the road as if waiting for someone to arrive.

Inside the tavern, Finn was met with the usual noise accompanying a room that held ten to fifteen drunken Scotsmen. The occupants seemed to be in fine spirits this evening. As Finn made his way to a table, he picked up bits of their conversation.

"I'd bet the lass wasn't *really* his wife. One can't get too far away from one of those, believe me, I've tried."

"…been out there all day long getting toasted by the sun while waiting for him to come back. As if he'd forgotten her."

"…she's a fine bit. I'll give her a place to stay for the night."

Each comment was met with laughter and it didn't take long for Finn to realize they spoke of the lady he'd passed on the steps.

The innkeeper brought his meal and a tankard of ale.

"Anything else for ye, my lord?" the man asked. Finn didn't bother to correct the address. There was not much graceful about him other than his title. He was a large Scot, and despite his untarnished heritage most people stepped to the side when he came close. As if he'd pull a claymore and remove their heads like a proper Highland warrior rather than a well-educated peer of the realm.

"Nay," Finn answered the man who turned to walk away when Finn's curiosity got the best of him. "Excuse me." The man stopped again. "The woman sitting outside…?"

He didn't need to do more than prompt the question while in his homeland. Scots didn't need much encouragement to tell a person a story.

"Aye. She's been out there all day long. She arrived last night with a man who said he was her husband, but I doubt that was true. He ran off this morning and left the lass here."

"I see," Finn said while wondering what kind of scapegrace would do such a thing to a lady. He focused on his meal. The woman was not his concern. He only wanted to get home.

Surely, she needed to go back to London, and Finn was heading in the opposite direction. Someone else would see her safely home. It was for him to take on. But as he finished his meal, the comments became increasingly worrisome.

"…her husband might have broken her in last night, but I'll be showing her how a real man goes about it."

"She doesn't have a coin to her name. I'm sure she'll be up for anything to earn a bit of blunt."

Finn paid for his meal and stepped out of the inn to find his coachman had his carriage waiting with four new horses to finish out the trip.

The woman was still sitting in the same place, still looking down the road with her chin propped on her palm.

As he passed the lady on the steps, he heard his sister's voice in his head.

"Help her, Finn," she ordered in that scolding tone only an older sister possessed. His steps slowed, but he didn't stop.

He, of course, knew he wasn't hearing his actual sister from beyond the veil, but his own conscience had taken on her persona. It seemed fitting as the lass was always telling him what was right and wrong when she'd lived.

While he'd eaten, he'd come up with every excuse as to why he should just go on his way and not interfere in the matter, only to have his sister's voice turn him around with one imaginary command.

"Wouldn't you have wanted someone honorable to help if it was me sitting there?" his Juniper-voiced conscience asked.

"Bloody hell," Finn whispered to himself as the coachman stood next to the open door. He was so close to being away from here, and any responsibility he did or didn't want to take on. But he knew he'd never stop Juniper from pestering him if he didn't do something. No, not something.

He needed to do the right thing.

He turned to face the bedraggled woman on the steps.

⸻ ◦ ⸺ ❀ ⸺ ◦ ⸻

Chapter Three

"PARDON ME, LASS, but are you quite all right?" Finn asked the woman, hoping for all he was worth that she would simply tell him she had everything under control and he could be on his way without guilt haunting him.

If luck were on his side, she would thank him for his concern and he would offer a nod and make haste for home to never think again of the woman's sable curls adorned with wilted primroses.

"I'm... I..." She blinked her large gray eyes at him as if she didn't know how to answer. Which seemed to be an answer in itself. He cast a longing glance at his carriage but turned back to the woman.

"I couldn't help but overhear the local men in the tavern speaking of your unfortunate situation."

She let out a mirthless laugh at that, which seemed to shake her out of her daze.

"Unfortunate situation?" She shook her head. "I'm afraid it's actually unfortunate *situations*," she said, enunciating the plural. "For the list grows on and on. The complete and utter destruction of my reputation is just one unfortunate situation. But so is the way I overestimated my ability to distinguish between an honorable gentleman and a lying, scheming, weasel of an arse. Definitely an unfortunate situation, that. But wait... there's also the matter of being abandoned in another country days from home without a bloody pence to my name. Which is perhaps the most unfortunate of all the many, many unfortunate situations."

It appeared the poor woman had gone mad. Perhaps from the shock, or maybe sitting out in the sun all day, as evident by her pink face and chapped lips.

Despite her discomfort, Finn noticed something interesting about the woman. Yes, she was quite lovely, as the bounders in the tavern had already noted, but while many damsels would be weeping mercilessly, in the face of these *many* unfortunate situations, this woman—clearly a lady, given her speech—was… cursing. She hadn't melted into a puddle of tears and hysteria. Or perhaps she had earlier in the day and he'd missed it.

Maybe his luck was intact after all.

Her stomach growled viciously and she pointed to her mid-section.

"You see! Yet another unfortunate situation to heap on with the rest. As I've not had anything to eat all day. When I get back to London, I shall have the blighter's heart served on a platter and feast upon it while laughing."

She was most definitely past any tears on the matter.

Despite her formidable imaginations, he didn't have the nerve to tell her that the unfortunate situations would become tenfold if she continued to sit outside a tavern filled with drinking men set on offering her a place to sleep.

"Help her," Juniper's voice came to him again. If his sister was really there, he would have had a stern word to say about getting involved in such delicate matters, as well as her bossing him around.

Instead, he just hissed in reply, "I am trying."

It was clear that his conscience wanted him to help this woman for he didn't believe in specters or visions. Especially ones that were not visions as much as hearings. There was no such thing.

"Blast and damn," he said under his breath for allowing himself to get caught up in an argument with…himself. What right did he have to think this woman mad when he was trying to puzzle out how to tell his dead sister to leave him be?

Without another word to her, he gestured for his coachman to wait while Finn went inside and requested provisions.

Back on the steps, he stopped and gestured toward the elaborate traveling coach with four fresh horses ready to finish his journey.

"Please allow me to assist." He stood at the open door with a flourish and waited.

She was back to blinking at him owlishly.

"I have food and we will arrive at my home in only a few hours where I will see you settled for the night. We can better determine our next steps in the morning in regards to your safe return to London, and the matter of the heart and platters and whatnot."

"I can't go with you," she said as if shocked he would even offer.

"Why not? You said yourself your reputation is already in ruin. You canna un-ring a bell." He wrongly assumed this logic would be enough to move her into the carriage so he could return to his home. For she didn't move, except for the crinkle of her forehead.

"But I don't even know you," she stated as if this explained everything. In certain circumstances it would have suited, but not in this dire situation.

He was unsuccessful at hiding his irritated sigh, as he looked up at the darkening sky. If his sister was anywhere, he imagined her being up in the heavens, so that is where he focused his look of displeasure before he continued on.

"One might argue that it doesn't matter if you know me or not since you've already admitted to your lack of distinguishing friend from foe. How long did you know the lying, scheming...er..."

"Weasel of an arse," she supplied helpfully.

"Ah yes, him. How long did you know *the weasel* before deciding it was safe to travel hundreds of miles away with him, only to realize you were wrong?"

Again, this logic didn't seem to meet her approval either if her drawn brows were any indication.

Rather than continue to wade through nonsense when he only wanted to get home, he cut to the heart of the matter.

"In another two hours, mayhap three, the men inside that tavern will be full of drink and feeling lusty. And they are going to come through that door on their way back to whatever hovel they crawled out of, and what will they find waiting for them, but a slightly sun-singed lady all but served up to them. I am a gentleman, and while not all gentlemen are honorable, I am one that is. So, will you please get your arse in the coach so we may be on our way?"

She stood and picked up her small bag and reticule, but before she allowed him to help her into the conveyance, she paused.

"Just one thing, if you wouldn't mind. I need to leave a coin for the maid who helped me dress this morning."

"No. Get in."

"Well, it surely isn't her fault I made a most hideous mistake by trusting the wrong man and might, at this very moment, be making an even more hideous mistake to leave with you. If it's the last thing I have any control over, I'd prefer to see her settled for her service as is only right."

He pressed his lips together tightly as he reached into his waistcoat, pulled out a guinea and held it out, pinched between his thumb and forefinger.

"Hurry."

She tossed her bag in the coach before snatching the coin and running back into the tavern.

"I hope you are happy, Juniper. Not another word. Do you hear me?"

"Who are you speaking to?" his most recent annoyance asked as she returned from her business inside.

"No one."

"Are you mad? I don't have the strength to deal with yet another unfortunate situation today, sir."

"I'm not mad," he assured her, though he didn't feel quite sane about this undertaking either.

He helped her into the carriage and got in across from her, handing over the food and drink he'd purchased as the coach began to move.

She took it and then proceeded to burst into tears.

"Bloody hell."

Chapter Four

H OW RIDICULOUS IT was for Lily to cry now, when she was safely ensconced in a luxurious carriage, and hopefully on her first step to getting her life set back to rights.

This man must think her a lunatic, and after she'd just questioned his sanity when she found him speaking to himself…

She had been talking to herself for most of the day. Well, not talking so much as scolding.

As she'd sat there baking in the sun, watching for any sign of Reggie's return, the facts taunted her. Reggie's insistence that he loved her and wanted to marry her after only sharing a few dances and a kiss on the terrace at the Waltham's ball was clearly a lie.

She'd responded to the kiss as the dry earth soaks in the rain, so desperate was she for anyone to pay her the slightest bit of attention. She'd then agreed when he'd suggested they elope so they could be married without her father coming between them. He'd told her he wanted her to be his wife as quickly as possible because he couldn't wait to start their life together.

And then he'd left her.

Not just left, he'd taken every cent she had, as well as the diamond necklace her sister had given her when Maribel's husband had decided the stone was too small for a viscountess.

Lily had been ruined and abandoned by a scoundrel, and was robbed of her things, as well as her dignity. And now, instead of going home where she would likely be tossed out, she was traveling further into the seventh circle of hell that was Scotland.

For the moment at least, she seemed to be safe and she had food and water, which was enough to overwhelm her with gratitude. She managed to stifle the remaining tears for the man across from her seemed more than uncomfortable. She worried he might throw her from the moving carriage to get away from a crying woman.

She practically guzzled the cool water and then remembered her manners. Or at least a few of them, she imagined she would still be prone to cursing for some time. At least any time the memory of Reggie came to mind.

"Thank you..." Oh, dear. She didn't even know this man's name. Perhaps she should just call him her savior, or knight in shining armor, but she preferred to give it some time before making such a claim. She had been incredibly wrong recently. "What is your name, sir?"

"Finneas Lockhart, Duke of Granton."

"Apologies, Your Grace. I am Lady Lily Cantrell."

"*Lily?*" He looked heavenward and rolled his eyes. "Of course."

"What does that mean?"

"Nothing. It appears my sister is playing a prank on me."

Lily didn't understand, but then it was clear from the predicament she was in she didn't understand much when it came to men. Despite having shared a womb with one, even Maxwell often times confused her.

However, one thing was becoming extremely clear. Men would do anything to have sex. No matter how dubious or dishonorable. She'd heard Max and Matty speak on the subject incessantly and now her assumption had been proven correct by her encounter with Reggie—the ferret-faced weasel of an arse.

Men were not to be trusted. Even handsome dukes who

seemed kind enough. She studied the man sitting opposite her and wondered if he was guilty of the same crimes. He was a man after all. Though his striking good looks and wide, strong shoulders put him out of her grasp, not that she would be grasping any men for the foreseeable future.

But the duke had done what seemed to be an honorable thing, unless he thought to get her to his home and reap some reward for his chivalry. If so, he was going to be disappointed.

She hoped his sister would prove a loyal friend, and help her navigate this impossible situation. For she truly didn't know what she was to do next.

THE WOMAN, LADY Lily, was comfortably quiet for the next hour or so. He wasn't sure if she was still numb from her trying day or if she was just a quiet person naturally. He appreciated the company of people who didn't feel the need to fill any wisp of silence with meaningless chatter.

His thoughts went again to Juniper and her endless babble. When she'd passed away, the castle had fallen silent, uncomfortably so. Which was why he'd decided to go to London, but he didn't find any peace in London either. It was exhausting, always needing to be aware of possible manipulations of marriageable misses.

He looked over at Lily and wondered if she had attempted to manipulate an elopement with the blighter who left her in Scotland without a care as to what happened to her.

He'd watched her when he told her his name, more importantly his title. He hadn't seen her eyes widen. Drool hadn't dripped from her jowls at the mention of him being a duke as he'd seen happen during the Season. Metaphorically, of course, because ladies didn't drool in good society and this one specifically wasn't in possession of what he would refer to as jowls.

Still, Lily showed only remorse for having called him a sir. A matter he didn't need to be corrected. Under the weight of his title and responsibilities, he was a man not unlike any other.

Well, perhaps he was different than the weasel arse who'd left Lily stranded in the inn where he'd debauched her.

Lily.

He still couldn't believe that was her name.

His sister's favorite flower. Juniper loved all manner of flowers, as their mother had, but she painted lilies most often because she favored them.

"What is your favorite flower?" he asked his traveling partner as they grew nearer to *Gealach*. He had opened the curtains on both sides of the coach to let in the soft light of the moon as they traveled north.

It touched her face and gave a blue cast to her dark hair. She was lovely, not that he needed to notice such a thing. She was no more than another responsibility, picked up along the way to be managed tomorrow.

She gave his question only the barest thought before answering almost immediately.

"Roses. Maribel says they are the only flower worthy of giving."

Finn nodded at her answer, though he didn't agree. For years, he had sat while his mother and sister worked in the gardens. He'd come to admire many different blooms for either their color or fragrance. He found roses to be overrated and fussy.

Lily's brows pinched together. He didn't know for sure, but he felt she regretted her answer.

"And Maribel is?" he prompted. Not that it was important for him to show any interest in her life, or the people in her life, but they would be traveling a little while longer.

"My apologies, Your Grace. She is my eldest sister. A viscountess."

"And roses are *her* favorites. Are they yours as well?"

"Oh, quite. I find their scent..." Her sentence rather drifted off. He worried she'd fallen asleep, but he could still see the moonlight reflected in her gray eyes, so he knew they were open still. "Actually, I find their scent to be overpowering, if I'm being honest. And they seem not to last very long. They begin to wilt almost immediately. But they are the most coveted flower, are they not? Any suitor worth a lady's time had better show up on her doorstep with roses if he wishes to make a good impression with the Cantrell household."

She fell into silence again, but he found he liked hearing her honesty so he nudged her again.

"Then roses are *not* your favorite. What is *your* favorite, Lady Lily?"

"It seems it should be lilies, does it not? But I don't think that's correct." He watched as she fretted over coming up with an answer. He didn't mean for his inquiry to cause her such a burden, but before he attempted to end the discussion her face fairly lit up.

"I believe violets are my favorite. They are not usually brought by a suitor, but I prefer them to not be picked. There is a place in the woods near our country home in Cornwall, where violets grow along the ground, so thick they look like a carpet of purple blooms. And purple is my favorite color. I'd thought it was blue, like my sisters, but I realize now I prefer purple, despite it being a color of half-mourning."

"I also like purple, though after the deaths of my family, I will say I am growing tired of it. We have heather here in Scotland. It also grows like a purple carpet across the hills. It will bloom in July. And the scent is quite lovely as well."

She nodded and smiled as if quite pleased with herself as she whispered, "Violets, yes." A few moments later she looked over at him and said, "Thank you for asking, Your Grace."

He only nodded. It was a simple thing. But it seemed significant to Lily for some reason. He didn't push for more because the sound of the carriage wheels on gravel foretold of their arrival home.

When the carriage stopped, the door opened. He stepped out and reached for Lily's hand to help her down. She blinked up at his home and swallowed.

"My, it is a castle."

"Aye."

The servants came forth to start unloading his things, despite the late hour. He and Lily met a surprised Mrs. MacDougal on the steps to the foyer.

"Mrs. MacDougal, this is Lady Lily, she will be visiting with us. Please put her in the Violet Room. Have a cool bath brought up as well as a glass of wine. She has had an exhausting day, and it will help her rest. Also check with the cook and ask if that salve she uses for burns would help soothe Lady Lily's tinged skin."

"Of course, Your Grace. I believe it might."

He turned back to Lily. "Do you read?"

"I do," she answered.

"Oliver, there is a copy of *The Tales of Bristol* in my study. Would you get it for Lady Lily?" He spoke lower to her. "It has put me to sleep each time I've attempted to read it, so I think it might be just the trick this evening for you."

She smiled and he felt the earth tilt. Perhaps not the earth, but at least the foyer where he stood. She was a lovely woman, as he'd noticed a few times during their journey despite the dim light. But here in the foyer, with a smile on her lips, he was caught off guard by her beauty.

Beautiful or not, she had gone through a stressful ordeal and he'd not add to it by gawking at the woman. She would not be in his home long enough to warrant noticing her lovely smile and intriguing eyes.

"Is there anything else you require for the night?" he asked, hoping to see his responsibility fulfilled.

"I believe you have thought of everything, Your Grace. I thank you for your valiant rescue this evening."

"I hope you will be comfortable in my home during your stay. If there is anything you need, please let Oliver or Mrs.

MacDougal know."

"I should be fine. Good night, Your Grace."

"Good night, Lady Lily."

He watched as Mrs. MacDougal led Lily up the stairs toward her room.

Oliver cleared his throat.

"She's lovely, Your Grace." He paused and waited for Finn to look at him before speaking again. "Does the lady not have a companion or a maid to accompany her on this visit to a bachelor's home?"

Oliver was not such a stickler for propriety. The man was simply trying to ascertain what situation had brought Lily to *Gealach* Castle.

Finn was not accustomed to lying to his staff. He felt for all the responsibilities rested upon his shoulders it was his reward to live however he wished without feeling a need to hide things from his butler. And Finn was not known to live far outside of propriety, regardless.

But in this, he would preserve Lily's reputation as best he could. And not just because it was not his story to tell.

"Through no fault of her own, Lady Lily became separated from her travel companion. I have offered refuge until other arrangements can be made."

He wondered how long those arrangements might take.

As he went to his study to have a drink, he found himself hoping she would not need to leave so very soon. He found himself curious to get to know her better. But of course, he would not.

It surely wouldn't be a quick thing to get a lady on her way back to London. He would simply offer her refuge until her family could provide safe passage for her return home. In the meantime, he would keep his distance.

The castle was so large, he doubted he'd even see much of her in the interim.

Frowning at the family portrait hanging in his study, he focused on the impish grin on Juniper's face.

"Yes, you would be quite amused, sister. I daresay, you would not have your fill of mocking me anytime soon."

‹‹‹❦›››

Chapter Five

"T HE DUKE REQUESTED the Violet Room for ye, miss." The housekeeper opened a door midway down the long corridor. The large woman bustled inside and soon the lamps were lit.

Lily stepped inside and gasped at the lovely room filled with paintings of violets. The drapes were a deep purple while the bedspread was a cheery lavender.

"It's beautiful."

"Miss Juniper did each of the rooms in a different flower. The duke must have known your preference?" the woman asked with wide eyes.

"He asked me before we arrived. I didn't know why he'd asked."

The housekeeper smiled and patted Lily's hand softly with a look of pity on her face.

"You poor dear, the sun has near to scalded ye. Nothing a cool bath and some of Mrs. Feather's balm won't ease."

Lily doubted even the highly-esteemed Mrs. Feather's balm would fix everything wrong in her life at the moment. But a bath would be welcome.

She would be glad to scrub the filth from sitting along the road all day, as well as whatever remained of Reggie's touch, from her body.

"Did you need anything to eat?" Mrs. MacDougal asked.

"No, thank you. The duke saw to my meal earlier."

"He's one for taking care of others. Took good care of his sister, he did."

"Where is his sister now?" Lily asked.

The woman frowned.

"She passed more than a year ago. The duke misses her so. Of course, he doesn't say it, but we know. They were very close."

Lily nodded, thinking the duke lucky in that, among other things.

She had three older sisters, and two brothers, and she wouldn't say she was close to any of them really. Of all of them, she'd spent the most time with Matty, the youngest, while they'd been younger. But of late, he'd taken to going to the gentlemen's clubs with Max.

He surely didn't seem to miss her with all the excitement of gaming and drinking available.

She smiled at Mrs. MacDougal as the tub was filled.

"Thank you again for seeing to me. You must wonder what has happened to bring me to your doorstep all alone." Lily thought she should explain, but had no clue what she might say.

Mrs. MacDougal patted her arm and shook her head.

"It's not my place to wonder and it's not my doorstep. Besides, dear, you weren't alone, now were ye?"

She hadn't arrived alone. She'd been introduced and treated as a guest by the duke.

A tap on the door brought the butler with the book the duke had sent for her. He must have known how her mind raced with thoughts that did her no good now.

"Do ye need help with your bath, miss? It's been a while since I've served as a lady's maid, but I know how to use a towel."

Lily laughed at the charming woman.

"I will be perfectly fine." She looked at her small bag thinking of what was inside. The thought of even looking at the night rail she'd worn last night when she'd been with Reggie made her feel ill. Both of her gowns were dirty from traveling, but she would manage.

The woman must have noticed her gaze for she said, "I'll get you a fresh nightgown from June's room. I'll bring a gown for tomorrow and we'll see your gown cleaned."

She felt tears well in her eyes again, as she was overwhelmed by the woman's kindness. She hoped Mrs. MacDougal wouldn't come to learn of Lily's shame. She didn't want to disappoint the woman like she would surely disappoint her family when they learned what happened.

Lily undressed and slid into the tub. A swift knock at the door made her breath catch, but it was only Mrs. MacDougal returning with the garments she'd promised.

"A good night to you, my lady," she said and was gone before Lily could respond.

Lily guessed it was a better night than if she had stayed at the tavern. She shivered at the thought of those drunken men. If the duke hadn't come along…

Sinking into the cool water, Lily slipped under the surface where everything was quiet. Not that it was loud in the room, but it was peaceful underwater. The frightening thoughts seemed to scatter and disappear.

She waited until she had no choice but to sit up and breathe. Her body instantly rejoiced with the intake of air.

Perhaps if she could just focus on breathing, everything else— the mess she had made of her life and reputation—would somehow work out. It seemed the only thing she was capable of at the moment.

Breathing out and back in.

"LADY LILY IS quite lovely, Your Grace," Mrs. MacDougal said as she entered his study. "She is all situated in her room for the night. I saw to her bath and the balm will certainly help her poor, reddened skin. I took her one of Junie's night rails, and a clean gown for the morning. I hope you don't mind."

"Nay. If Lily can put them to use, she is welcome to them." He imagined she wouldn't want to wear the gown she had planned to be married in ever again. And giving her Juniper's gowns meant he wouldn't have to have them cleared from his home in some awkward, emotional, event. "Thank you for seeing to her, Mrs. MacDougal."

"I don't know what happened to bring her to *Gealach*, but it could be a blessing for you to have some company, Your Grace."

He raised a single brow at his impertinent housekeeper.

"She will not be staying long." Though he doubted she would be on her way the next day. It would take a few days for her to send word to her family and for them to send a carriage to collect her. She would be under his roof for a month at least.

"Mayhap we should send to the village for someone to serve as a chaperone while she is here," he suggested. He was to understand from Lily's initial rant that she had been compromised, so a chaperone was not going to change anything that had already happened. But a proper guard would serve to protect him from an eager father wanting to marry off his ruined daughter to the person who offered solace.

"I will speak to Olly about it. I know of a few ladies who would be eager for the work."

"Not Beatrice," Finn snapped. The girl had been a companion to his sister and was always floating around with a dreamy expression when he was nearby. He'd overheard her tell Juniper she hoped to be Finn's duchess someday. He surely didn't need to deal with disappointing the woman.

Mrs. MacDougal simply smiled her rosy grin and dipped a curtsey.

"Good night to ye, Your Grace."

"Good night, Mrs. MacDougal." He thought to warn the

woman from any meddlesome machinations she was considering before she'd even begun, but he found he wasn't up to it.

It was late and traveling drained a person. Though Finn didn't understand why. It wasn't as if he'd pulled the carriage himself. He'd only sat inside. What reason did he have to be exhausted?

As he made his way to his bed chamber, he gazed down the hall toward the guest quarters. He knew exactly which room was filled with paintings of violets. He imagined Lily sleeping under the lilac bedding with her dark hair trailing out across the pillow.

How lovely she must look.

He shook the thought away before entering his room and closing the door. It wouldn't do to think of Lady Lily in that manner. She'd had an ordeal and only a weasel of an arse would think of such things when she was dealing with such heartache.

For it was clear, despite her obvious anger, that she'd been deeply hurt by such a betrayal. Finn didn't know who the man was, but that might be for the best. For if he knew who had done such a horrid thing to her, he just might find himself across the dueling field with a pistol at the ready.

Perhaps it was this anger that caused him to be restless all night and rise much too early for someone who had returned home so late the evening before.

He was already finished with his breakfast and was going through the post when Lily entered the morning room.

He stood and greeted her properly with a bow.

"I hope you slept well given the reading materials I provided."

She smiled and he felt his chest tighten at the sight.

"Yes, thank you. I slept much better than I expected."

He gestured toward the sideboard laden with all manner of food. Mrs. Feathers always overdid things the morning he first returned home to *Gealach*. He guessed it was her way of welcoming him back.

Today, however, it seemed to be prudent, for Lily piled her plate with food.

She ate quietly as he read the post, casually watching her when it was safe to steal a glance.

When she was finished, he set the mail aside and steepled his fingers.

"I imagine you wish to return home to London directly?" he started the conversation he couldn't put off any longer. She had a life to get back to and no doubt worried parents to comfort. And he had…well, nothing of note.

There was always the care of his estates, reviewing the books. But he had a trustworthy steward to handle things and rarely needed to question anything he did.

He could go for a long ride. Mayhap he could assist the groom with the birth of a new foal.

The fact that he liked having someone to share his morning meal with was not her concern.

But as he watched, expecting her to show relief to be offered a way home, to put this error behind her and move on with her life, he was surprised when she winced and bit her lip nervously.

"Is something amiss?" he asked, knowing he would do whatever was needed to clear such displeasure from her lovely face.

"I wonder… That is, do you know how one might go about finding employment as a governess?"

"You wish to seek employment as a governess?" he asked foolishly for, of course, she was speaking of herself.

"I don't wish to, but after my reckless error, I'm not sure my parents will allow me to return home. It would be best if I had an alternate plan ready if it were to become necessary."

He blinked at her and she smiled nervously.

"I understand that might sound strange coming from the person who waltzed headlong into ruin not two days ago, but one should learn from one's mistakes. If I return to London to find I've been cast out, I will need to find a way to support myself."

In truth, Finn should have considered such a thing. It was probably a common threat used against young women to keep them in line and out of such trouble as Lily had found herself in recently. But would her parents really turn their backs on her after a mistake?

"Do you not have any other family who would take you in if it came to that?" he asked, though it was none of his business.

Lily pressed her lips together for a moment as if considering his question.

"My eldest sister, Maribel, is twelve years older than me. We were not very close as I was only five when she married the viscount. She would never cross my father by taking me into her home. Martha is a countess, and ten years older than me. She lives in the country with her five children and has not visited or even written in many years. Millicent, a baroness, who is eight years older than me, would gladly cheer my parents on as they tossed me from the steps. My twin brother, Maxwell, only thirteen minutes older, is too busy being a rake and dragging my younger brother, Matthew—eleven months younger—into his debauchery."

She shrugged as if it was acceptable for a family that large to not care about their sister in her time of need, but Finn was caught on something else.

"All of your siblings have names that start with the letter M?"

"Yes."

"But you do not?"

"No."

That was the only answer she gave. Yet, that one word somehow served to explain things she hadn't said. She was different from the rest of her siblings. An outsider among her own family. He knew it by the way she was content to sit quietly and not need his attention.

The anger he'd felt for the man who'd taken her away from her home radiated out to encompass a family who didn't treat her like the strong, beautiful woman he'd seen in their short acquaintance.

"I don't presume to order you about, but I would rather not

send you back to London until we could be certain you have a proper home. Until we are sure, you will stay here as my guest."

That last part had come out exactly as the order he'd said he wouldn't presume, but he didn't want her to even think to leave under the pretense of being a bother.

While he didn't wish to lumber about in this huge castle with only his sister's disembodied voice for companionship, he wouldn't turn to her for companionship. For she would not stay long. He would allow her to stay until they received word from her family that all was well and she would leave.

She twisted her lips to the side and then her gray eyes lit up.

"I can write to my brother and ask him if I will be well received upon my return. Then I will know better what to do next."

"Aye. That is a good idea." And if he truly thought it a great idea because of the time it would take the post to deliver and a reply to be sent, he kept that to himself.

Chapter Six

WITH HER LETTER to Matty written and sent on its way, it seemed there was nothing left to do but wait for a reply.

Lily walked next to the duke as they strolled the garden. It was a chilly day, as early May should be. Not like yesterday when she'd felt as if the fires of hell had already had her in their grip.

The duke told her how his mother loved flowers and had shared that love with his sister. The fondness with which he spoke of his parents and sister nearly brought tears to her eyes. She hurt for this man who had been part of such a loving family and was now all alone in this big empty castle.

In many ways they seemed opposites. His parents had clearly adored their children. While she was often forgotten. She'd seen the look of pity in his eyes when she'd confirmed she was the only child of the marquess whose name didn't begin with 'M.'

She could only imagine how much worse it would be if she'd told him how that had come to be. And before she thought to do it, she opened her mouth and began speaking.

"When Maxwell was born, he was taken out to my father who, I'm told, nearly shouted from the rooftops that he had an heir. He was so pleased to have a boy, he didn't realize my mother had given birth to me as well. My mother told me he went straight to his club to share the news and didn't actually find out he had another daughter for a few days. My mother had always liked the name Lily but my father was steadfast with naming his children with an "M" after him. So, she named me Lily in what, I later realized, was probably spite."

"It is unique then. Special."

"Yes." But if he thought her name or even her dark hair and gray eyes would make her stand out among such a herd of blond-haired, blue-eyed, perfect children, he would be wrong. She needed to change the subject.

Here with the duke, it was just the two of them. It seemed odd to have someone's direct attention without having done something wrong to earn it. She found she rather enjoyed talking with him. A real conversation.

"The violet room is quite lovely. What other rooms are there?" she asked because the duke's amber eyes seemed to light up when he spoke of his sister.

He held his arms out wide, gesturing toward the flowers around them.

"Pretty much every flower represented out here has its own room inside the castle." He smiled before asking. "Do you wish to try them all?"

She laughed at such a thought.

"I would like to see them, but I'm quite comfortable among the violets."

"I will give you the tour this afternoon. While chilly, it's a pleasant day, would you join me for luncheon by the lake?" He paused and then added, "It is well in the shade."

She brushed her finger over her nose, where her skin was still tinged pink from her exposure the day before. What a difference a day made.

Yesterday she was miserable, heartbroken, and angry, and today she was strolling with a duke and laughing.

She didn't know how she might thank him for what he'd done for her.

She glanced over at the tall man walking next to her and once again noticed how handsome he was. Maybe not handsome in the way Reggie was, that lying ferret, for the rake was brimming over with dimples and charm. She saw such things now for what they were. Bait to lure in unsuspecting women who were desperate for anyone to notice them and pay them the smallest attention.

How pathetic she was.

The duke had stopped walking and it took her a few more steps before she noticed.

"You are thinking about him," the duke said while nodding toward her hands which were clenched into fists. She released them slowly and then shook them out.

"I feel like such a fool. Not even a month into my first season and I fell for such an obvious trap."

"Your first season?" he asked, that pinch of confusion between his brows she was coming to know.

"Yes, though I'm two and twenty. I should have known better."

"Why was this your first season?"

She welcomed the exchange of one uncomfortable subject for another.

"My mother takes to times of melancholy and has been unable to launch me into Society until now."

"Surely your other sisters could have stepped in."

Lily shrugged, realizing how tragic she must seem to someone who had been part of such a loving family. She decided she would rather speak of Reggie than have the duke look upon her with pity.

"I am wondering if I was the first woman to fall for this trick or has the rotten oaf lured other women to their demise with that same ruse."

The duke sighed. "I imagine if he was such a skilled liar, he has had at least some practice."

"You have not asked his name."

The duke grinned at her.

"I rather enjoy hearing the names you create for him. I fear his actual name would be dull in comparison."

She smiled at that, but a moment later, he gave a more serious answer.

"I don't know so many Englishmen, I spent much of my time here at the castle until my sister passed. Of the men I know, I certainly don't know any so disreputable to do such a thing to a lass. I feel speaking his name gives him an honor he doesn't deserve. For now, at least, he shall only be known as a feckless sow."

She giggled at the new name.

"Thank you, Your Grace. Your kindness gives me faith not all men are so horrid. The truth is, I am not normally so careless. I have always been a good daughter."

"All the more reason your parents should afford you this misstep. Everyone makes mistakes."

She didn't think the duke capable of mistakes. He surely hadn't made any thus far in her opinion. He was actually quite perfect. And handsome.

She clenched her fingers into fists again, but this time it was in anger at herself. She was still entangled in a horrible scandal because she had allowed a man to blind her with his charms, and here she was getting dreamy-eyed over the duke. Because he'd done little more than be a decent human being.

No one was perfect, not even the duke. She would not allow herself to fall into another trap. Not ever again.

The tour of the castle took the rest of the morning. Not only were there a copious number of rooms, but they had turned the tour into a game in that she was to guess which flower would be found behind each of the doors.

She hadn't guessed correctly. Not even one time.

"You are quite horrid at this. I'm sure you will guess this one, since it is your favorite flower, or at least you believed it to be initially," the duke said with a crooked grin.

"No fair. You're not to give hints," she scolded but he only laughed.

"If I don't give you a hint, I fear you will not get even one correct guess."

Hamming it up, she placed her finger at the corner of her lips and squinted toward the ceiling.

"Let me think. Could it be hyacinths?"

"Now you're being obtuse," he teased as he opened the door to what was clearly the Rose Room. Large cabbage roses took up the fabric on the draperies and bedding. A number of paintings of roses were hung about. Some showed roses blooming on a bush, while others showed them cut and displayed in a vase. The walls were a deep pink and the rugs were a deep red.

"This is quite atrocious," he said. "I feel like I can smell the stifling scent of the blooms by just looking at them."

"You don't like roses, Your Grace."

"Too much time spent in ballrooms with women who drenched themselves in the smell." With a mock shiver he pulled the door shut and nodded to the next room.

Lily pressed her lips together thinking of what flowers they'd seen already. Maybe using the process of elimination would help. They'd seen daisies, and marigolds, and black-eyed Susans. There'd been lilacs and irises, and primrose. She knew it wouldn't be violets because they hadn't reached the room she had stayed in.

"Pansies?" she guessed with a wince.

His eyes seemed to shift from amber to green as his lips pulled up in a smile and he opened the door with a flourish.

Paintings of pansies filled the room.

She squealed with delight and even executed a little hop and clap.

"Well done, you."

She stepped inside and admired the paintings.

"Your sister was very talented. All of these paintings are so beautiful."

He nodded, but said nothing.

"I'm sorry if talking about her is painful. Forgive me." She couldn't imagine being so close to a sibling as to think of them as one's dearest friend and then to lose them.

"Nay. It is actually nice to speak of her. It's just…" he trailed off. She thought he might not say any more but eventually he continued. "Her paintings came about when she became ill. So to me, I remember feeling like I was losing her when all she could do was sit in her bath chair and paint."

He moved past the next two rooms and opened the one at the end of the corridor. The room was filled with paintings of white lilies on light green walls. The drapes were a soft yellow and the bedding was white. And next to the window sat a wheeled chair with intricate carvings. Of course, the duke would have had the most beautiful chair commissioned for his dear sister.

An easel and a tin of paints still sat by the deep-set window.

"I used to sit in here while she painted and we would talk about all manner of things. Occasionally she would have a seizure, and for some time, I paused upon entering because I didn't like being there when she had a fit. She was always exhausted afterward and I would worry she would not wake up again."

Without thinking, Lily reached out and put her hand in his, giving it a soft squeeze to show her sympathy. When she realized what she'd done, her breath caught, but before she could remove her hand, he squeezed her fingers back and she heard the words he did not say aloud. *Thank you.*

"I wish I had such a strong tie to any of my siblings. We've never been close like that. I didn't know to miss such a thing. But now I do and I find I miss something I've never had. How silly."

"My sister would mock me relentlessly for saying this, but I have no patience for the silly activities of the ton. It was why I left London so early in the Season. It all just seems so insignificant. The balls, the card games, so trivial."

"I understand. I am two and twenty, quite old for a lady to

come out, but as I said, my mother was otherwise engaged in recent years and there was no one to escort me to events, so I waited. All the time I waited I was certain I was missing something of great import. The man that was supposed to be mine could have been attending a ball at that very moment and meeting someone who wasn't me. I thought I was missing out on everything my life was supposed to be."

"Were you?"

"No. When I attended my first ball, I found it quite boring. The lemonade was not even good." They laughed. "And I was supposed to agree to dance with anyone who asked, even if I had no interest whatsoever in the man. In truth, it felt like a waste of time. As if my life was passing by and this was the thing I had to do until I met the person I was meant to be with. So I could finally start living."

"Yes. I too, feel like I'm in stasis, waiting to start living again. Though I've moved around from here to London and back again, hoping to find the thing that will push me into living."

"And then you found a stray woman sitting on the tavern steps and she has certainly ruined all your plans."

He shook his head.

"No, Lily. While I wouldn't have wished this heartache on you, it has at least given me a purpose for the moment. So I thank you for needing me. No one has needed me in some time."

Their hands drifted apart and Lily missed the warmth of his palm against hers. How silly she was thinking of a man like that after what had happened. Had she learned nothing from her fall from grace?

Men could not be trusted. Even kind men like the duke who seemed surrounded by sadness. And even worse, she could not trust herself. She was not above having her vision clouded by a few sweet words and a warm touch.

She needed to be more aware of her weakness, so not to fall prey for another man's tricks.

$$\text{Chapter Seven}$$

"WOULD YOU BE interested in taking our noon meal out by the lake? It has turned into a lovely day, I feel we should enjoy it," Finn suggested. The spring in Scotland was a fickle thing. Days that were almost overwarm followed by a frigid chill. And then days when there were both.

Lily nodded. "That sounds nice."

They had left Juniper's room, and Finn hoped to move on to happier topics. Not that thinking of Juniper was unwelcome. But he didn't want Lily to find him morose. Even if he was.

He found Mrs. MacDougal and told her of his wishes. She assured him everything would be ready within the hour. Lily went to her room to ready herself for the meal and Finn went to his study to see to any mail that had arrived.

No doubt in the next few weeks he would receive a missive from the Marquess of Devon with news regarding Lily's fate. He hoped the man was not one of the bullheaded louts he saw in the House of Lords who cast dispersions on anyone who didn't do as they aught.

He, a married man, who had a mistress, if Finn had deciphered Lily's unease correctly, would turn out his own daughter for being lured into a situation by a man who'd promised marriage? Finn would have something to say about that if it came to be.

Juniper had always complained about the different set of rules for men and women. What he was encouraged to do, she was not allowed to do. At the time, she'd been speaking of climbing trees and wearing breeches. But she would have found this situation to be similar.

Men were encouraged to sow their wild oats, but where exactly were they to sow them when women were to remain virtuous until marriage? Finn had never visited a bawdy house. He'd seen what could happen when a man trifled with the wrong lass.

Finn's first experience had been with an older woman from the village who'd taken a liking to him. And the few women he'd been with since had been widows looking for comfort and someone to warm their lonely beds for an evening or two.

But Lily made one mistake in trusting someone who had made promises and she was considered ruined. Her father would have trouble finding her a husband if the story got out.

Oliver knocked at the door.

"Everything is set up at the lake, Your Grace."

"And Lady Lily?"

"She has just arrived downstairs."

Finn nodded and got up. He would have to solve the world's problems another time.

He offered his arm and led Lily out to the small table and chairs that had been set up for them. The light meal was served on their arrival and the footmen left them to eat in quiet.

And it was extremely quiet.

The woman was silent, abnormally so. Or at least it felt it should feel that way. In truth, he didn't feel any irritation or resentment coming from her as a cause for her silence. It just seemed she was a quiet person.

Having listened as she spoke of her family, he heard more of what she *hadn't* said.

Being the fourth daughter with a large age difference between them would have most likely been enough of a reason to have been ignored. But to have been born minutes after the marquess's heir, she had surely been born directly into the shadows. And that shade had probably grown dimmer still when the spare was born only months later.

Finn thought it explained why Lily had maybe jumped at the chance to find happiness for herself, and why she had not employed enough caution to save her from scandal.

While sitting next to her as they enjoyed the mild day, and the picturesque view of the lake, he felt comfortable in their silence, but still, he found himself speaking.

"You are very quiet, and coming from me, that is something to be sure. I am usually the one accused of being uncomfortably silent."

"I'm sorry. It's certainly not the company." She offered him one of her enchanting smiles and he wondered how the arse had been able to walk away from such a lass. He'd surely never find anyone more lovely.

Perhaps now that her anger had faded, she was feeling the pain of having her plans to wed tossed aside. Did she miss the man who'd betrayed her?

"Are you thinking about what has happened and what to do next?" He couldn't bring himself to ask if she was thinking of him. For some reason he feared his reaction if she was pining for the man.

"Maybe. A bit. I believe it is common to return to an event in one's mind, and think of how one might have done something differently. Even though there is no sense in such things. There's nothing to be done now. As you so elegantly put it, one cannot un-ring a bell. It is over. It has happened, and now I must forge ahead as best I can. It doesn't help that I don't know yet if I will be welcome in my home."

"Yes. I understand."

"I can't imagine a duke has many regrets."

"I would have agreed with you years ago. I guess I'm having

trouble finding my feet now. I should have built other relation-ships. I have my friends, of course, Shay and Reese are quite entertaining. But perhaps it's time to marry and start my own family. Though the thought of taking on such an endeavor seems tedious. And I fear my loneliness would make me less discerning."

She nodded.

"I see now that was a big part of why I was quick to run off with the ferret-faced arse. I was desperate for someone to see me. To want me. I fear I fell for his ruse completely because I so much wanted to believe he loved me. Now, as I sit here gazing out over this lovely view seething and hating him, I realize I didn't love him at all. How could I with his ridiculously hideous laugh? He sounded like a young girl being eaten by an orangutan when he found something funny."

Finn could not help but to laugh at her description of the man.

"See, now that is a fine, manly, laugh. I'm not worried I'll be called upon to save a child from a primate attack."

They were both laughing in earnest now. He found her laugh to be lovely as well. The sound was filled with joy. It made him feel lucky to be near her. And her humor, especially in spite of all the reasons she had to mope about was endearing.

"My sister would have enjoyed your sense of humor," he said, wondering if he had laughed so hard since Juniper had died. She was always able to make him laugh and often did things to make him spit out his drink at the table. Earning them both a stern look from their parents. "You must think me a sot for moping about my sister as I am. It's just, she was my very best friend. I knew it when she was alive, but maybe not to the level as I realize it now. I fear I took her for granted in the way one does when they didn't tell the other person how special they were."

It was odd that this strange woman whom he didn't know well at all had already made him feel more at peace than anyone else had since June passed. He would keep that to himself so not to frighten the poor woman.

"I have a rather large family, though we are not close, it is something to just know they are there. I had always thought it good to know I had someone I might depend on if I were to need them. But now that the time has come, I find I'm not sure what I should expect from them. This might be too much."

She shrugged as if she knew she could do nothing to change their minds. He hoped her family saw her as the joy she was and would welcome her into their open arms to comfort her from her heartache.

"I can't speak to how your family will respond to your predicament, but I can tell you if I had the chance to have my sister back, ruined or no, I would be there for her no matter what."

"I guess we will see. It's times like this that will test the bonds of family."

"Indeed."

The clouds grew dark just as they finished eating so they walked quickly toward the house.

"We can finish our tour if you are up for seeing the rest of the castle," he suggested, not wanting to leave her alone. He knew well how being alone made a person think more than they should on things they had no control over. He wished to spare her if he could.

"Yes. That would be lovely. So long as I don't have to guess anymore. I was horribly bad at it."

"You won't have to guess." He stopped at the room across from the ballroom. "This is the music room," he said as he opened one of the double doors. He expected her to peek inside and they could then move along, but she stepped inside, her gray eyes alight with excitement.

"Do you play?" she asked him.

"Nay. My sister and my mother did." He watched as she traced a slender finger over the polished wood of the pianoforte. "Do you play?" He guessed she did by the interest she showed in the instruments.

She shrugged as he was learning she did often when she wished to cast attention away from herself.

"I am proficient."

"Will you play something for me?" he asked.

As if she was glad he'd asked, she slid onto the bench and tested the keys for a moment. Tilting her head to the side as if confirming it played correctly.

He was prepared to tell her she played beautifully regardless of her talent, for it was clear enough Lady Lily had not been given enough compliments in the past. But as she began, he knew there would be no need for false pleasantries. She did play beautifully.

Heartbreakingly so.

The piece was complex with a slower, somber song winding inside a faster, lighter melody. The fingers on both hands were a blur as she moved across the keys with something exceeding mere proficiency. She was a master.

Even more impressive was she played such a complicated piece with no music. The composition rose higher and higher and he felt his breathing had picked up, so caught up in the sounds her fingers made. And then it fell to a few simple, soft notes and he blinked away the stinging sensation in his eyes.

He clapped with gusto and after he cleared the tightness from his throat, he said, "Your modesty was misplaced, Lady Lily. That was far more than proficient. I have never heard anything so amazing in my life."

Her cheeks tinged pink and she looked away. He was set on breaking her out of such an impulse. Perhaps her family didn't understand what a treasure she was, but he already had in this short time.

"If it pleases you, perhaps I will play in the evenings."

"I will definitely take you up on your offer. This castle has been silent for far too long. How did you come to play so well?" Her skill was far beyond what young ladies usually learned from a music instructor.

"I have had plenty of time to practice as I waited my chance to attend a season." She rose and went to the harp. Taking a seat, she settled the instrument into position and began to play. Once more he was in awe of the sounds she managed to coax from the strings.

When she finished playing the harp, she picked up the flute sitting on the table and played a merry tune. But one he didn't recognize.

She moved on to the guitar, and after a few strums and adjustments of the tuning knobs, she plucked a gentle melody that filled the room with its resonance.

She reached for the lyre, and after playing something lovely on that instrument as well, she all but rushed to the place where the violin waited as if for her hands to wake it from its long rest. The sound as enthralling as it was as she played the others. When she finished, she smiled at him.

"The flowered rooms are lovely, but I do think this room is my favorite," she said with an impish grin.

"You play everything." Before she managed to lift her shoulders, he said, "Don't shrug off such a talent, Lily."

She pressed her lips together, but the smile broke free.

"In truth, I have not played to my fullest potential in front of anyone before. At least not for a long time. When I was younger and would try to impress my family with my playing only to have them talk over my efforts or ignore me completely, I decided it was easier if I didn't expose my own creations to such indifference."

It took him a moment to understand.

"Your own creations? You mean you composed all those songs."

"Yes." With a nod, she added, "Just now."

"Just—you created such beautiful music while you played?" When she nodded again, he was nearly speechless. "Someone given the opportunity to practice such compositions for years would not have been able to play them with such skill. You have a gift, Lily."

"Thank you. I'm glad you enjoyed it."

"Enjoyed it? Nay, I was moved by every note you played."

She stood and came to stand next to him as if she was ready to continue on with the tour of the castle. As if she did not realize she'd touched his very soul with her music. While he felt as though he'd been awakened from a dark slumber.

"Thank you," he said simply, though it was not nearly enough.

"Of course. I will be happy to play for you during my stay. Might we consider it a small repayment of your generosity?"

He understood the need for one to rise above charity and make their own way, and would not deny her a way to offer value in exchange for her stay. So rather than explain how unnecessary it was, he simply said, "Yes. That would be a fair exchange."

Lily all but beamed at him and he worried he had risen from his slumber into uncertain waters.

* · — · ❦ · — · *

Chapter Eight

L ILY FELT AS if she were walking on air as they left the music
room. It was well equipped with all the finest instruments.
She looked forward to playing for the duke in the evenings.

It was clear His Grace enjoyed listening to her play. She was
guilty of trying to impress him. She'd not played for anyone who
so openly appreciated her skill.

Flattery and empty promises were the reason she was staying
at *Gealach* Castle in the first place. She was more careful now to
watch for such pretenses. But she felt the duke was sincere in his
admiration of her playing. And she certainly wasn't in danger of
falling into bed with the man because he'd been swept away by
her compositions.

She was well on guard now. No man would catch her una-
ware again.

But while she was here, waiting to hear back from her family
and learn her fate, why couldn't she enjoy her time here? If she
was going to end up living at someone else's estate as a governess, she might not get another opportunity to play simply for the
fun of it.

A bit of worry turned in her stomach, but she pushed it away.
There was no sense to start fretting over her future now. There
was nothing to be done one way or the other. All she could do

was wait.

Her father was rather absent most of the time. Either at his clubs or spending the nights elsewhere when her mother was not in residence. All the times her brothers had been caught up in mischief it had been brushed over with a few minor grumblings from the marquess and then it was done with.

But she had never done anything to earn his ire. She'd always made certain to be a model daughter. Especially after following in her sisters' footsteps. They were the epitome of grace and deportment and Lily had tried to mimic them when she was younger.

Now she knew them to be harsh women. Matty called them shrews and while she hadn't admitted to agreeing with him, she couldn't say he was wrong. They spent most of their time gossiping about whichever sister was not in attendance. Usually it was Martha as she preferred to stay in the country even during the Season.

After hearing the way they greedily picked the flesh from any woman they deigned unworthy, Lily assumed she was the one being devoured when she wasn't with them.

What a tasty morsel she would make for them now.

When the tour had concluded she'd made her way back to the room of violets. She sat on the wide window seat and looked down into the gardens where they'd spent the morning and remembered the morning before when she'd woken in the tavern and thought her life was about to bloom.

Everything looked different to her now. Especially herself. She was no longer a silly girl hoping for love with no sense as to where she and Reggie would have lived or what they would have done for funds. Now she thought of practical things. Like how she would provide for herself if her family were to cast her out.

Being a governess would provide a place for her to stay. But maybe after she'd saved up enough she could become a music instructor. That might make her happy.

If there was anything she'd learned from her colossal misjudgment it was that happiness was secondary. All that truly mattered was survival.

She would find a way to survive this.

AFTER SPENDING THE afternoon in his study seeing to things and being distracted by thoughts of his houseguest, Finn went to the formal dining room for a late meal.

When Lily arrived, he assisted her into her seat as any gentleman would, but he found himself bending closer to catch the scent of oranges in her hair. No cloying rosewater for Lily. He wanted to ask her where she'd gotten such a lovely perfume, but it wasn't his business. And it was much too personal.

A man did not ask about things that touched a woman's body, whether it be a gown or an exotic smelling oil that he imagined had offered a cool kiss before warming on her skin.

Shaking his head to rid himself of the intoxicating scent, he woodenly found his way to his own seat and all but plopped into it. Fortunately, the footmen served their meal and the savory notes of lamb roast chased away the citrusy smell of temptation.

"Will you tell me more about your sister?" she requested.

It hadn't been a subject change as they had not been speaking on any specific topic when she arrived in the dining room, but the topic was still an abrupt deviation from where his mind had been.

"Aye. What would you like to know."

"Was she older or younger than you?"

"Older." He hoped she wouldn't ask how much older. He wasn't ready to go into that. Not until he was certain Lady Lily wouldn't cast any judgement. He didn't think her the sort to bandy about words like bastard. If she were, she surely would have employed the use of the word when describing the fool who'd used her so callously and then abandoned her. But still, he wasn't ready to expose this detail of his family.

While he'd never been ashamed of Juniper, many thought she should be hidden away as his father's dark secret. The fact Finn's mother so easily accepted Juniper in her home as one of her children was often the topic of gossip in the village.

Finn imagined it was also the reason Juniper never went to London, and had refused even the slightest suggestion of having a Season.

"Did she remind you often that she was oldest?" Lily asked with a smirk on her lips.

"I do believe they teach such things to older sisters the moment they are out of leading strings," he said, making light of a conversation that had the potential to turn grim.

He understood the kindness Lily revealed in offering him the chance to speak of his sister. Many people, upon hearing of a loved one's death, chose to talk about anything but the person who was lost. As if speaking of them would cause pain, and not speaking of them was a way to avoid that pain.

When, in fact, not speaking of them caused its own type of pain. And speaking of them eventually became easier and while not effortless, it was a comfort.

"My sister loved flowers as you have seen during our tour today. But she also loved animals. She had a few horses, two dogs, and a plethora of barn cats in her keeping."

"Dogs? I love dogs. I have always wanted a dog, but my mother and father refused, saying they didn't wish being stuck with the care of it. As if my parents would have personally cared for anything. They didn't even care for their horde of children." She frowned, and after wiping delicately at her mouth with her napkin, she looked up at him with a wince. "Forgive me. That was rude. I'm obviously still ruffled about not getting a dog."

Finn laughed when her lips broke into a smile. It was all the sign he needed to know she was jesting and it was safe to break into laughter.

"Now that you mention it, Father refused to let me keep an injured squirrel I'd found and I'm quite miffed about it still," he shared.

"How rude of him to stop you from catching some dreadful disease from a wild animal. Parents. So cruel. It's a wonder we have made it to adulthood with any social graces."

He liked the way she'd lumped them together in her remark. *We.*

"Speak for yourself. I'm a Scot after all. Most Londoners find us barbaric."

She casually waved her hand. "I do not mind the way you eat with your hands and snarl over your meal, Your Grace."

He found himself laughing again as he used his fork and knife to cut into his food and place the tiniest bit into his mouth, as was proper when dining with company.

"You jest, but if you were not here, I would have devoured this by now." He pointed to his plate with his knife. "I still would have used cutlery, but I would have taken much bigger bites instead of nibbling my meal to death."

She covered her mouth as she laughed.

"It does seem to take forever to finish a meal with such small pieces. I often worry I will fall asleep before I am done."

"I beg you not to fall asleep tonight, for I'm very much look-ing forward to hearing you play after our meal."

Her cheeks turned a lovely rose and she nodded before taking a sip of wine.

"Do you have any requests?"

"Nay. Only that it be something you've created. Anything would be welcome."

"It is easier to play something I've made up, no one can ac-cuse me of playing it incorrectly."

He chuckled but wondered if Lily had ever played anything incorrectly in her life. She seemed at one with the instrument when her fingers were moving across the keys, or strings for that matter.

When the meal was over, he assisted her from her chair.

"Do you take port with the men after your meal, Your

Grace?"

He chuckled, not only because there were no other men in their party tonight.

"Port? We are in Scotland, lass. We drink whisky here."

"I see. So barbaric." She was teasing him. Nay, as he looked down into her sharp, gray eyes, he saw she was *flirting* with him. Probably something that came as easily to Lady Lily as playing the pianoforte.

When had their pleasant banter turned into something else? Something so dangerous?

He guessed there was a fine line between the two. Perhaps no difference at all really, except for the look in one's eye when a phrase was delivered.

There was definitely a look in her eyes.

He should have backed down and turned the conversation to safer topics. He could have not returned her jests. He could have even left, so not to encourage any future pursuits. What he shouldn't have done was deliver a response in a low voice with a flirtatious look in his own eyes.

"Do you wish to be barbaric with me, Lady Lily?"

"Yes," she whispered, and he felt the word melt through his body, warming every chilly corner of him. He leaned closer to her, before realizing he was on the path to kissing her, and abruptly pulled back. Something that seemed to take not a little bit of effort for his body resisted his mind.

Clearing his throat, he looked away and bid his blood to cool. With a nod, he led her to the music room, where he poured them each a glass of amber liquid, hers slightly less than his own for he didn't want to turn the girl tipsy.

They were already playing a dangerous game, it was best to keep one's wits about them.

Sitting at the pianoforte, Lily began a happy tune that turned slower and eventually grew in depth of both note and feeling. She played for nearly an hour, ending with a piece that made his throat tighten and his eyes burn with unshed emotions yet again.

How did she do such a thing to him? It wasn't sadness. But a passion so deep he felt he had been irrevocably changed.

She finished the song and emptied the last sip of whisky from her glass. He saw the concentration it took for her to set the glass back where it had been.

He'd not wanted her drunk, so he'd only served one glass, but of course, she wouldn't have been accustomed to such strong spirits. Her slight body must have drawn it up like a sponge. Not to mention she didn't have the inherent constitution for whisky because she wasn't Scottish.

"I do believe I must beg a reprieve. My fing-hers are not working quite right," she said with a giggle.

"Oh, dear," he muttered, though he couldn't help but smile at her slight slurring of the word "fingers."

He helped her up from the bench and supported some of her weight as she swayed.

"My apologies, Lady Lily. It was not my intention to set you in your cups. I'll help you to your bed." He nearly froze when he realized what he'd said. Lily simply giggled again. "What I mean to say, is that I will provide escort to your room and you shall go inside on your own."

"On my own," she repeated as if saying the words again would help them penetrate the cloud of whisky surrounding her brain.

What had he done?

By the time he got her up the stairs, after some bit of stumbling and leaning, and to the door of her room, he realized he would not be able to leave her at the door. Not unless he wished for her to spend the rest of the night out in the hall.

Opening the door, he quickly took her inside and put her in bed. Actually, gravity did that, for he just stood her next to the bed and she fell over on top of the pale lavender bedding.

He'd been right when he'd envisioned her the night before. Her dark hair did provide an enthralling contrast against the fabric.

Shaking his head, he turned to leave, but realized her legs and feet still hung over the bed in what he assumed would be an uncomfortable angle after a few hours.

He picked up her legs, noticing how his large hands wrapped around her dainty ankles as he turned her to fit on the bed. Looking down at the slippers on her feet, he decided he should remove those. For the purpose of comfort, of course.

He gave them a slight tug of her heel and the first shoe slid off. Her stockinged feet were so tiny in his big hands. He couldn't help himself from giving the first a squeeze before turning to the other.

With her shoes removed and her now sleeping completely and soundly atop the bed, he backed away toward the door, feeling as if turning away from the sight of her would cause him some great amount of pain.

In the corridor he breathed in deep, the air seemed to release him from the spell.

"Good God," he muttered and wiped a hand over his face.

She was too beautiful, too funny, too talented, too intelligent, and too beautiful. Christ, he'd already thought that.

He was growing much too comfortable with Lady Lily. He'd hoped to provide safety as he would have done for his sister, but in less than a day, he'd abandoned any brotherly feelings for her. He was already being tempted.

His blood heated in the presence of her smiles and laughter, and when she'd played for him, he felt the intense stirrings of passion.

He'd wanted to offer safety, but now it seemed, he was becoming the danger instead of the champion.

A chaperone could not be found quickly enough.

— ⟡ —

Chapter Nine

L ILY WOKE IN the dark of night unsure of where she was. It took a few moments for her to make out the violets on the walls and remember she was at *Gealach* Castle.

With the duke.

The impending fear faded away at the thought of him. His light, brown hair a mix of browns and golds. Not unlike his eyes that blended green with amber. As if one color wasn't enough for such an important man, he needed to have a thousand shades to encompass the richness of his character.

My, she was feeling a bit muddled. And why was she still wearing the gown she'd worn to dinner?

How had she gotten into bed? She remembered playing for the duke while sipping the drink he'd poured for her. The end of the last song had taken every bit of concentration she could muster in order to finish and then the room had swayed when she opened her eyes.

The whisky.

She'd not drank anything but wine previously, and had enjoyed the smokey deep flavors of the whisky. She hadn't been prepared for the effects.

Curling her toes, she noticed her shoes were missing.

Had the duke removed them? Had he touched her?

Again, the stirrings of fear skidded away when she pictured the duke touching her ankles. Did she want him to touch her?

Thoughts of touching suddenly took a turn when she pictured him touching other parts of her. From her ankles, to her calves, to her thighs. She recalled the way she'd felt that night with Reggie.

The way feelings of want had grown and seemed to spin out from her core. Threads pulling tighter and tighter as if something grand were about to happen. But when nothing had, she'd felt rather disappointed. No...*frustrated*. Even irritated by the weight of Reggie's suddenly still body squashing her. She had shoved him off and he'd only grunted at the disruption before falling asleep.

That grunt had been the last thing he'd said to her. In the morning he'd been gone.

Closing her eyes in the already dark room, she tried to push the memories away. She had wanted every moment of what they'd done, but now she realized it had been such a large price to pay for something so unfulfilling.

She couldn't help but wonder now if it would be different with the duke.

My, but the whisky had turned her mind to mush. Getting up, she went to the pitcher and poured a glass of water followed quickly by a second. She went to the window and looked out over the garden where they'd walked that day. The beautiful colors were muted by the night and shadows cast across the space.

She couldn't help but feel at home here. This place she'd spent little more than a day gave her peace she never felt at Devon House or the family's London townhome.

She didn't think this feeling had anything to do with drink, and everything to do with the man asleep in the duke's chambers at the end of the hall.

What was wrong with her? When had she become so fanciful? Having given her body to a man who'd paid her a few nice compliments, now she was thinking of the duke in much the same way because he'd been kind to her.

Was she doomed to be a wanton creature like her mother who was not so discreet about her many affairs? Even worse, her father was much the same way, seeking entertainments with his mistress instead of his wife.

Perhaps Lily should find her way to the nearest convent so she wouldn't be able to give in to her inevitable destruction.

Yanking off the gown, she got back in bed wearing only her shift and pulled the fluffy covers over her. If she was destined for the harsh environs of a convent, she would enjoy such luxuries for the moment.

Then she recalled something she'd heard her brothers speak of. Something far worse than any fate at a convent.

They'd said fallen ladies often ended up in brothels. At the time, she'd not understood what it meant to have fallen. She had an understanding of what a brothel was. Or at least had an idea from the way they spoke of going there.

She now knew what it meant to have fallen. She was a fallen woman. Would she end up serving men in a brothel?

She thought of what she'd done with Reggie that night and imagined having to do that with strangers every night. Fear surged through her body drawing her muscles tight.

Never in all her life had she expected to be in such a situation.

While her mind seemed set on flipping through every un-wanted thought, her body claimed her to sleep. She relented more quickly than she would have expected considering her rampant thoughts, and slept soundly until the birds outside her room woke her with their song.

She managed to dress herself in one of the loaned gowns and put up her hair in a tidy bun. As she went to the breakfast room to meet the duke, her feet seemed to want to hurry, all the more quickly to see him.

She tried to convince herself it was only because she was terribly hungry, however she knew that wasn't true. Not only because her stomach was slightly unsettled from the drink the night before, but because the man was beautiful. And more than that, he was a good person, though endearingly gruff at times.

She paused outside the room and gave herself a stern talking to. Silently, of course, but a reprimand all the same about proper decorum of a lady. And how she may have been spawned by randy and disloyal parents, but it didn't mean she had to give in to such depravity.

She would be all that was respectable. She thought briefly it might be too late to be respectable having been ruined just a few days past, but starting now, she would be nothing but respectability.

As soon as she walked into the room and the duke looked up at her with a smile, her stomach flew into a riot of butterflies and her pulse picked up its tempo. Her body flashed hot, especially the one place respectable ladies did not think of, where the heat seemed to focus and throb.

She offered a strained smile in return and took her seat quickly before he could even get to her to help her. She couldn't allow him to come so close to her when she was in this state. She feared she might grasp hold of him, like some wild beast in rut.

And they'd jested about how Scots were thought to be barbarians.

"I trust you slept well? Are you feeling yourself this morning?" he asked.

"Yes, thank you. I apologize for my state last night. The whisky seems to have gotten away with me."

He chuckled, the warm sound seemed to reach out and wrap itself around her. That place throbbed again. Why, oh why, had it awakened today with this man? It had slumbered even as Reggie fumbled about her breasts and lower body. But just a smile from the duke and she nearly melted to the floor in a puddle.

"You were not so deep in your cups. I've been far worse. At least you were able to get to your room under your own power."

"Oh, good." She didn't admit that she didn't remember any of it past leaving the music room. Had she been leaning on him? She closed her eyes for a moment so she might push that thought away.

With a slight nod, she looked away to focus on her meal. Perhaps if she didn't look at him she would better be able to control her overpowering lust.

He said a few things, just idle chit chat. She offered the expected answers but didn't elaborate or attempt to draw the conversation out longer.

As soon as the food was gone from her plate, she excused herself and practically ran to her room to escape temptation.

It seemed her passions for the duke were growing out of control and she needed to squash them. She'd been wrong before with Reggie. And she was wrong now.

The duke especially would not be interested in her as a wife, having known her situation as he did. He was only being kind to the silly girl he'd found on his travels.

He did not want her. At least not for any respectable purpose. She would do well to remember that. She was ruined and if word got out, no man would ever want her.

$$\sim\!\!\text{❦}\!\!\sim$$

Chapter Ten

FINN FROWNED AFTER watching Lily—*Lady* Lily, for he needed to think of her as a guest and not an object of interest—flee from the table as soon as she finished eating. She'd been very quiet while she was in the room. Not the normal quiet he was accustomed to thinking of her. This was different.

His guest seemed tense. It was easy to discern by the way she'd speared her ham and eggs with more gusto than the staid meal deserved. Then she excused herself almost immediately after finishing.

Perhaps she'd felt the change in him the night before and she was making herself scarce because she was afraid of him. Not afraid in the sense of an attack, he'd given her no reason to feel threatened in that way. But she must have seen the way he'd looked at her.

The way a man looks at a woman he longs to touch, and kiss, and…well…much more.

Good God, she'd just been taken advantage of by a man pretending to love her, and here he was fairly in a lather for watching her play the pianoforte.

Perhaps it was this desperation to spare Lady Lily any further awkwardness that had him hire Mrs. Prichard as a chaperone only two minutes after she'd entered his study that morning.

He didn't worry over the woman's qualifications. If Mrs. MacDougal or Oliver thought she would do, he trusted she would as well.

The woman was rather stiff and slightly pinched about the face and eyes as if she was in constant danger of smelling something unpleasant, but she'd offered him a tight smile after he'd proposed she take the position, and he felt the relationship was off to a good start.

Besides, even if he didn't grow to like the woman at all, it wouldn't matter for she'd not be in his home all that long. A few weeks, a month at the most, and then Lily's family would send for her and she and the new chaperone would be gone from *Gealach* Castle.

And he'd be alone once more.

If his stomach tightened at this information, he paid it no mind and went on about his day.

Or tried to, until Mrs. MacDougal bustled in and waited for him to address her before speaking.

"I see you've hired Mrs. Prichard," his housekeeper said.

"Aye. Isn't that what you expected after sending her to me?"

"I wasn't the one to find her. Olly did. So if she doesn't work out, I want it noted I am not at fault."

"Do you have reason to think she won't work out, Mrs. MacDougal?"

"Only that she is rather high on the hill, Your Grace."

"I had noticed she was older, but I'm not asking her to win a race at the games or compete in a caber toss. She's only to watch over a guest."

"Nay, but people might question her use as a chaperone. Especially as she is in your employ. People might think it plausible that she be directed to look away since her livelihood is dependent upon pleasing ye, Your Grace."

"Good lord. It isn't as if Lily has the funds to employ her own chaperone. She needed a chaperone and I have provided one. What else am I to do?"

"I think you've done all you could, Your Grace. Mayhap just see that the woman stays awake when she is supposed to be looking after ye."

Finn couldn't stop from rolling his eyes. He worried he was hanging on by a thread of propriety. Just a few more smiles from Lady Lily and he would plummet into disgrace. If he needed to employ a sharp stick to prod Mrs. Prichard into protecting her charge from his interest, then he'd do so.

"Thank you, Mrs. MacDougal."

When his housekeeper left, Finn slouched in his chair and let out a breath.

"'Tis only a few weeks. A month at the most."

LILY'S FIRST WEEK at *Gealach* had gone by with relative ease. Lily still felt overheated when she noticed the duke watching her as she played each night, but having refrained from drinking anymore whisky, she did not require assistance going to her room.

Each morning Lily sat with equal parts eagerness and terror while the duke flipped through each piece of mail received that day. Who knew a duke received so much correspondence? Every day he managed to get through the pile and shake his head, Lily felt both forlorn and sparred. She was suffering quite the jumble of emotions.

Wanting to know her fate, while not wanting to miss a day here with the duke. Not wanting to overstay her welcome, while wishing she could stay there the rest of her life. She switched between a medley of feelings numerous times a day.

It was still early, perhaps her brother had yet to get her letter, or mayhap he had and was in the process of locating and interrogating their father as to what should be done with her.

It was daunting to think that at this very moment, her fate

might be being decided in London while she was there with the duke.

The duke had kept his distance these last days and she did the same as well. Perhaps both of them understood the risk her loose morals posed.

Mrs. Prichard was a compact woman who wasn't much for conversation. She generally sat quietly in the corner of the room with her knitting when she wasn't snoring. Given her age, Lily didn't wish to startle the woman to her death, so she often allowed the woman to sleep while Lily went off to do other things.

Mostly she stayed to the music room, quietly playing the different instruments, and imagining how they might all blend together if played at the same time. She coordinated different melodies and layers of music for each instrument.

Other than stopping by for a quick greeting, the duke had not requested her company for lunch by the lake or laughed with her over dinner. He was the picture of nobility, and she hated it.

Sitting at the breakfast table with him in silence was nearly more than she could take. But she let out a sigh and focused on eating even if she had lost all taste for her meal. And the day, and her time here at *Gealach* Castle.

"I'm sorry you are disappointed. I'm sure you will receive word soon. Mayhap tomorrow."

Without thinking she shook her head.

"I am not disappointed," she said when, in fact, she should have allowed him to think that was the issue.

He cocked his head, curiously. Silently asking her what was amiss.

She chose to provide him with a partial answer.

"I imagine I am used to being in London with an event each night. While I normally enjoy the country, I find myself thinking too much with no other distractions." She shook her head. "Please ignore me, Your Grace, I sound like a spoiled girl, when in truth I am so grateful you have given me a place to stay while I wait to hear word from my family."

He let out a breath not unlike the sigh she regretted.

Picking up the post again, he flipped past a few letters before stopping and holding one up toward her.

"This is an invitation to a dinner party at the vicar's home in the village. I was planning to decline, but mayhap we should attend. It would get us out of the house and allow us the opportunity to converse with other people."

"Would they not wonder how I came to be a guest at your home?"

"Whether is it right or wrong, you will find not many people contest the word of a duke. If I tell them you are a friend, and they see you are properly chaperoned, they will accept it as truth. And as matter of fact, it *is* the truth. I do count on you as a friend."

A friend.

She should have been squealing with joy for an event to attend as well as having the duke admit to thinking her a friend, but for whatever reason she now felt the disappointment he'd accused her of moments ago.

She could not want more than friendship from the duke. Or rather, she shouldn't.

The fact he only saw her as a friend should also give her some bit of relief that even if she were to let loose with her feelings, he would surely clamp them down directly and set her back. She could trust him to keep them in line.

Chapter Eleven

TWO EVENINGS LATER, dressed in the gown she'd worn when she left London, she arrived with the duke at Mr. and Mrs. Haywood's fine home. The duke had said it was a dinner party, but there was also a group of musicians playing in the corner of the large drawing room and an area had been cleared away to allow dancing before the meal.

It wasn't uncommon for country hosts to employ similar entertainments as were attended in Town.

The duke introduced Lily and Mrs. Prichard to a number of people who stared at her curiously, and nodded in approval at the duke's explanation on how she'd come to be standing in their home.

As he'd said, no one challenged his account, or asked her any additional probing questions. It was simply accepted that she was his friend and nothing more.

As they drifted away from the other guests, they took a spot at the edge of the room where she could see a few couples on the small dancefloor.

When a new dance began, she was surprised when a lanky young man came to bow before her.

"Would you do me the honor of standing with me for the next dance, Lady Lily?"

"Oh," she said, wanting to do anything but dance with him. But, of course, it would not be acceptable for her to turn away an offer from a gentleman, so she nodded and gave the duke a desperate smile. "How lovely," she said to the boy as she took his offered arm and he escorted her to the floor.

They turned and spun with the other dancers as he chatted about a number of inane things. Things she would have found intriguing when Reggie had spoken to her during their few dances.

Had it taken so little for her to fancy herself in love with the bounder? She hadn't provided the slightest challenge to the ferret-faced weasel. She'd fallen so easily for his charm. How naïve she'd been. But no longer.

She smiled when it was appropriate and engaged in polite conversation, but she used her demeanor to communicate that was all he would be getting from her.

When he returned her to the duke, he bowed and hurried off.

Beside her, the duke chuckled, a low sound that vibrated throughout her body.

"You find something amusing, Your Grace?" she asked pointedly while staring at the dancers rather than him. She knew if she looked at him, she would see that devilish grin. Perhaps if he was particularly entertained, he would smile wide enough to allow the dimple on his right cheek to peek out.

She nearly melted when that dimple showed itself. So, she didn't look. She couldn't afford to melt this evening.

"I don't know what you said to the lad, but he looked a bit pale as he scurried away."

"I didn't say anything. I was the picture of politeness."

"All while giving him a look that told all you were less than impressed with him."

"I'm afraid I am not so easily impressed as I once was. I see these men for who they are. I can guess at their true intentions."

He gazed down at her with his eyebrows raised.

She frowned. "Was it so obvious?"

"Maybe it was only me who noticed since I was watching you so closely."

What did he mean by that? He'd been watching her? Closely?

After days of dormancy, that heat curled slowly through her bloodstream, her heart pumping it along until she was fully consumed.

"You look overheated. I shall get us some punch," he said before walking away.

Lily fumbled a bit with her fingers as she waited for him to return. She looked across the room at Mrs. Prichard and wondered if it would be safer over in the corner.

Before she could move, she was greeted by a pretty young woman with shining black hair, blue eyes, and a smile that could only be called snide on her rosy lips.

"So, I am to understand you are friends with the duke?"

"Yes. That is true," Lily said cautiously.

"You are living with him." Her eyes fairly glinted with her statement that was not so much a question. But Lily answered anyway.

"That is correct. For the time being."

The woman's gaze drifted from Lily's toes up to her hair which Mrs. Prichard and Mrs. MacDougal had helped her with. Apparently, the other woman found Lily lacking for she shook her head. Just a slight movement that seemed full of judgement. So, it was to be like that.

Lily looked toward the table where the duke had gone for the punch and saw he'd been intercepted by another person on his way. Which meant he wouldn't be returning soon enough to save Lily from this woman.

"I'm Beatrice. I was a dear friend of the duke's sister, Juniper."

"I see," Lily said, though she did wonder how close this woman had been with the duke's sister as he and the rest of the staff always referred to the woman as June. It was rare to hear them use her full name.

"If you have designs on the duke, I should warn you that

would be unwise."

Lily felt her eyes widen at the woman's impertinence. She might not know every personal detail when it came to the duke, but she did know he'd never mentioned this woman.

It would have been petty to say as much, but when the woman looked down her nose at Lily, she found she no longer cared if she was being petty.

"Odd, he hasn't mentioned you at all. Are you close?"

That had hit its mark if the flare in her eyes was any clue.

"We will be very close when he has decided he is ready to settle down and marry."

"Hmm," Lily said. She couldn't speak to what the duke's plans were in regards to settling down, but something unpleasant fluttered along her spine at the thought of the duke taking this woman for his wife.

It was none of her business, of course, he was free to marry whomever he wished. But Lily thought of him married to a sweet woman with a kind smile and a wonderful sense of humor. The duke was funny, he needed someone who would laugh easily at his jests.

The duke came back handing over a glass of punch to Lily as he took a sip from his own glass.

"How kind of you to get a glass of punch for your friend. I was just making her acquaintance," young Beatrice said in a tone that reminded Lily of the beagle at her sister's home whose tail was always in motion with excitement to please his master.

"Hello, Miss Tanglewood. I hope you're doing well," the duke said formally.

The vicar's name was Tanglewood as well, so Lily assumed this woman was his daughter.

The girl trilled a laugh and reached out to put a hand on Finn's arm. Lily fought the urge to put a stop to the contact. And when had she started to think of the duke as *Finn*?

"Oh, Finn, you can surely call me Bea. After all, we're practically family."

The duke raised a brow that spoke volumes regarding his disagreement in that regard. Lily relaxed and shook off the small bit of shame she felt as the other woman dipped a quick bow and scurried away.

"That woman is the reason I never leave a room. I cannot tell you how many times she's contrived to get me alone. Once she even dropped out of a tree on me as I was making my way to the stables. She might have succeeded in trapping me if she'd not sprained an ankle in the process. She even feigned friendship with my sister to get closer to me. A more ruthless girl I've never met."

Lily felt her fingers pull into a fist. It was better she hadn't known this about the woman before she'd walked away for Lily might not have been so courteous.

And she wasn't sure which thing she found more repulsive. That she was attempting to trap the duke into marriage, or that she had used Juniper. Used her for her own gain.

"If I were not a lady, I would plant her a facer for being so cruel to your sister. It is the lowest of scoundrels who pretends to care for someone just to use them."

Finn must have realized where her thoughts had gone, for he offered a consolatory frown.

"I'm sorry that happened to you," he offered with complete sincerity.

"And I am sorry you have to deal with women falling out of trees in an attempt to become your duchess. Do not fear, Your Grace," she said while leaning closer to whisper, "I will protect you."

He laughed loudly enough to draw the attention of others in the room, including Miss Beatrice who scowled at Lily.

Lily lifted her glass of punch to her lips but the duke held her arm from rising farther and said quietly, "This punch has whisky in it, so drink it slowly."

Hearing it contained whisky had her wanting to toss it into the nearest plant, but she couldn't risk embarrassing the duke so she took the tiniest sip possible. She found the flavor of fruit mixed with the smokey warmth of the spirits enticing, but paced her sips so as not to need the duke to get her to her bed and take off her shoes tonight.

"Would you dance with me?" he asked, surprising her and doing nothing to stop the burning desire circulating through her body.

Again, she wished to say no, though not for the same reason she'd resisted dancing with the other young buck. However, Society forced women to accept any offer, no matter how dangerous. For when he touched her, she feared she might explode into flames.

"Very well. Let us dance."

As she placed her hand in his, she heard his laughter low and warm in her ear and a shiver went through her. Though she was not chilled.

No, definitely not chilled, she burned.

⸺⸺✦⸺⸺

Chapter Twelve

T HOUGH FINN WAS certain Lily had been disinterested in the young Mr. Fletcher, he saw none of that disinterest in her gaze now as she looked at him.

She might have wished to avoid dancing with him, but now that they were on the floor, touching, he saw only attraction in her gray eyes. Perhaps it was his own attraction reflecting back at him, but he didn't believe this was one-sided.

How arrogant he'd been to think he could handle being this close to her. He'd been able to avoid her at home over the last week, but now he realized how vulnerable he truly was.

Had he thought he was in control of his feelings? He was not. And now he would be at the mercy of the tiny, elderly woman sitting in the corner to stop him from doing something unforgiveable.

A woman who was watching them with bland enthusiasm. No, she was not watching. Dear God, she was asleep. Again. Had he really thought to entrust Lily's safety to this woman, who was prone to falling asleep in nearly any situation?

Fortunately, he was saved from any further misstep by the other dancers as they were pushed and pulled in different directions to complete the country dance.

Had they been in a London ballroom during the close confines of a waltz, he wasn't sure what might have happened.

He stayed where he was, watching as she danced with the other gentleman in the set. All were old enough to be her father and were married to other ladies in attendance, so there was no reason for his jealousy to flare as it had with Mr. Fletcher.

Not that he had reason then either. The lad had barely shed his spots and gangly awkwardness of youth, which made him an unlikely adversary. But Finn had felt the chill of irritation creep up his spine as the man had touched Lily.

Finn was nothing more than a temporary host. He had no say at all over who Lily chose to spend her time with. But jealousy was not a reasonable emotion. As proven by the way Beatrice flounced around the room with a cheery smile on her lips except when others weren't looking and she sent a scathing look Lily's way. He knew some men enjoyed the drama of women fighting over them like cats, but Finn was not one of them.

Although, it had warmed his soul to hear Lily threaten the woman and vow to protect him. Mayhap there was more to it than he'd originally thought.

Still, he knew it was best to stay on Beatrice's good side rather than have to look over one's shoulders at every turn.

When the dance concluded, the vicar announced it was time for the meal to be served. As the highest-ranking person in attendance, Finn was not surprised to find himself placed at the head of the table. Fortunately, Lily was seated next to him.

Finn managed to raise his glass in a toast to their hosts. Lily offered a nod and he smiled foolishly at her approval. Lord and Lady Doddle were seated across from Lily with Lady Doddle next to Finn.

He thought the woman had lost control of her feet until he felt the intentional climb of her toes up his leg.

Clearing his throat, he shifted his legs away from her attack and began conversing with the lady's husband. He hoped this would discourage her, but only a few more failed attempts to gain his attention finally stopped her pursuit.

Lily joined in the conversation, easily charming the man with her wit and humor. He wondered why she'd been left to the mercy of the arse who'd abandoned her. Why hadn't she been claimed by a reputable gentleman before the age of two and twenty?

She'd told him this was her come out. He guessed this delay served as proof to the *ton* she was somehow undesirable, when quite the opposite was true.

She was entirely too desirable.

He needed to get her another chaperone. Mayhap a whole battalion of them to keep him from doing something unfortunate.

When the meal ended, Lily stood with his assistance and he noticed the rosy glow to her cheeks. She'd been drinking wine with dinner but had only seen a footman refill her glass once.

"Don't worry, Your Grace. I'm not in my cups," she whispered, her warm breath touching his ear and neck.

Good God, he feared he would grab her up and kiss her right there in the middle of the dining room.

"Very good," he said with a smile. "Then I won't have need to carry you to the coach."

She laughed and took his arm to be escorted outside. A footman had awakened Mrs. Prichard and she followed behind them.

In the carriage, the woman fell back into a doze and he and Lily shared a grin.

"I'm not certain Your Grace is getting his money's worth in this arrangement."

"I am skeptical myself."

"It is an apt example of the ridiculousness of propriety, is it not? Having this woman here protects me from ruin, when the only thing I'm in danger from is getting her drool on my gown."

He laughed even though he knew that wasn't true.

The woman's presence, however unresponsive as it was, kept him from acting on his desire to pull Lily to his lap and kiss her.

Back at the castle, Finn helped Lily down and instructed the footman to help Mrs. Prichard to her quarters.

Lily stumbled on the stairs and he righted her, holding her tighter than was needed, but not willing to let her go.

"I assure you, Your Grace, I am perfectly able to get to my room on my own tonight. I am even able to remove my own slippers." She was teasing him, but he nearly growled for wanting the opportunity to take off her slippers again.

But he stopped at the head of the corridor near his rooms.

"Then I shall leave you to it and bid you a good night."

"And I hope you have a good night as well, Your Grace. Thank you for accompanying me to the dinner. You were a most gracious partner."

Partner. He thought of the long-forgotten words of his father, instructing him to choose a wife who would also be a partner to him in all the things life would bring.

Unable to speak, Finn nodded and waited for Lily to take her leave. But she didn't step away from him right away. That pause brought back all the lust he'd pushed down throughout the evening.

He wondered if his efforts to avoid her, avoid them, were futile. It seemed neither of them were strong enough to stop the inevitable. Did that mean they should simply surrender?

Why should they keep fighting something they both wanted so badly? He was hanging tightly onto the edge of sanity.

When she bit her bottom lip, he saw the flesh trapped by her white teeth because he had already been focused on her mouth. He leaned closer, captivated by her mouth and how lush her lips were. How soft her kiss would be.

She gasped and stepped back, breaking the connection.

Startled, he gave an abrupt bow and all but ran for the safety of his chamber. When he looked back, Lily had made it nearly to her room.

She looked over her shoulder to find him watching her. With a little wave, she slipped inside her room.

Without her scent clouding his judgment and her body so close to his he could feel the heat of her skin, he was able to think more clearly. Lily had trusted him enough to stay at his home.

To kiss her would only have led to more, and that could not happen. Even if they both wanted to explore what that could be. She had wandered down that path already and he would not be another regret for Lady Lily.

She had been strong enough to spare them for another night.

He worried how much longer that would be the case.

Chapter Thirteen

L ILY LEANED AGAINST the door in the Violet room, her chest heaving and her heart thumping. She had managed to stop the duke from kissing her. It was not difficult as the duke was an honorable man and would never force himself on her, she was sure.

The thing that had been remarkable was that she had stopped him at all. When she had wanted nothing more than to lean up and press her lips to his. She wanted to fall apart in his arms as he kissed her into oblivion.

And she knew that was what would have happened because she'd been kissed and lost all sense before with Reggie. Somehow, she thought it would be even better with the duke. His lips were full and curved enticingly when he grinned at her. Lips like those would know how to kiss a woman and make her lose all sense.

But then what? When the moment was over and awareness returned, what would happen? He would not wish to marry her. A fallen woman left in a tavern would not become the Duchess of Granton and bear the duke's heir.

She was nothing but a folly. Convenient.

He was attracted to her; she saw that in his eyes as the colors churned like an impending storm cloud. Gold and green battling for position.

But attraction would not be enough. He may be able to show her all the things Reggie had not. All those feelings that seemed to be leading somewhere only to fade away before realized. But what then?

After the passion, and she knew there would be passion between them, she would be alone and possibly broken into more pieces than she was already.

She'd managed to come through Reggie's betrayal with her heart intact if not her maidenhead, but she didn't think her heart would survive losing all she would give to the duke.

No. Not to *the duke*. To Finn.

If she had not learned anything else from her mistake with Reggie it was that she was worth more than a dalliance. She would demand better from the next man. And if no other man found her worthy, she'd pass through life alone, for she knew she was worthy of more.

The next morning, she found herself pausing at the breakfast room again. She expected some awkwardness after what had almost happened between them the night before.

What she hadn't expected was to find the room empty, but for the footmen who were standing at the ready near the sideboard.

Had the duke overslept? He'd always been in the room upon her arrival.

She spotted Mrs. MacDougal from the doorway and nodded at her.

"Have you seen His Grace this morning?" she asked.

The older woman pressed her lips together and nodded.

"Aye. He's already been down and gone. Says he has business to see to in the village today and that he won't be home before dinner."

"Oh. I see." For a fraction of a second Lily wondered if the business was a mistress. Had he turned to someone else after he'd not gotten what he wanted from her?

But Lily cast that thought aside for two reasons. One, the

duke did not seem like her father, and secondly, it was none of Lily's business what the duke's business entailed. She was only glad she was able to think of him as the duke again.

Back in the breakfast room, Lily ate her meal and then went to the music room to continue working on her piece. Throughout the day she found herself looking toward the door, hoping to find the duke standing there watching as he sometimes did. Urging her to ignore him and go on with her playing.

As if she could ignore someone so compelling.

She ate the noon meal alone as well and then dinner. And so it continued into the next day, and the next.

The duke was always busy, in the village, or checking the crops in the fields. Day after day he would leave before she had the chance to speak to him or even see him.

She took to asking after the post with the butler, but each day Oliver assured her no letter had arrived for her from her family.

Finally, after two weeks longer, Lily lost her patience. It was beyond clear the duke no longer wanted her in his home. If she left, he might feel comfortable enough to stay in the castle especially on days like today when the sky was heavy with rain.

Her presence in his home might cause the man to take a chill, and she would not have it.

Lily packed her small case and asked Mrs. Prichard to pack her things as well so she might escort Lily to London. The woman seemed to come alive with excitement and was quick to pack her bag as well.

She found Mrs. MacDougal and asked the woman to pack a lunch for them.

"Will ye be taking your noon meal by the lake today? It's a bit damp outside."

"No. I'll not be eating by the lake, I will need food for travel."

"Travel?" the woman asked, but Lily didn't stop to explain. She moved to the foyer and asked Oliver to have the coach made ready to leave shortly.

"And where would you be needing to go, miss?" the butler

asked.

"To London."

"London? But does the duke know you are leaving *Gealach*?"

"No. But since I have not seen hide nor hair of the duke for weeks, I cannot be sure he is not already in London himself. Regardless, it matters not, for I wish to leave. Can the coach be brought around for me and my chaperone, please?"

Oliver looked over Lily's shoulder and when she turned, she spotted Mrs. MacDougal looking back at the man with wide eyes.

Lily was put out by the servants. She understood why they would be loyal to the duke as they worked for him and she was no one of importance. Just a responsibility, a duty he took upon himself to allay a guilty conscience.

She would be his burden no longer.

"I was told by the duke I was not a prisoner here. I am able to come and go as I please. If you would please have the carriage readied and food brought, I will be on my way."

"You are not a prisoner, of course, but I do worry the duke will be upset if you were to leave and take his employee without him knowing."

"Very well, then. I will go on my own." She was ready to walk back to London if that was what it took, no matter how many months it might take. The housekeeper was right. Lily couldn't take Mrs. Prichard with her. Even if Lily could afford to employ the woman herself, she would need a nap before they got to the end of the drive.

Besides, Lily still had no money. She didn't know what she would do, but she would find a way. It was time to take her fate into her hands.

"I'm sorry, Mrs. Prichard, but you'll need to stay here as I do not have access to a conveyance. I thank you for your service and wish you well. As I do to you, Oliver, and Mrs. MacDougal. Good day."

With that, she gave them each a nod and walked through the door.

"My lady, I would ask you to wait to speak to the duke," Oliver called after her while looking back at the ladies as if begging them to do something. Both ladies merely stared back at him.

Lily continued walking down the drive.

"Wait," Mrs. MacDougal called a moment later and Lily, not wanting to be delayed with such a long journey before her, kept walking. The portly woman caught up to her, cheeks ruddy and out of breath and held out a bundle toward Lily.

"Here is some cheese and bread for ye. Please, be careful."

"Thank you, Mrs. MacDougal."

"By the way, I understand why you are sore with the duke."

"I'm not sore with the duke," Lily said, knowing it was a lie. "I just wish to be home."

An odd feeling lurched in her stomach. The feeling that she was leaving her home rather than going to find it. But this was not her home.

"Thank you," she told the woman and turned to be on her way without looking back.

As the rain pelted her face, she pulled her pelisse closer and kept on. She could only hope this didn't turn out to be yet another mistake.

$$\text{Chapter Fourteen}$$

"YOUR GRACE!" FINN heard someone call for him through the downpour that had started a few minutes earlier. He was helping the gamekeeper with some trees that had fallen on his property.

It was not his place to be laboring next to the man, but it was a distraction he welcomed. He searched for anything that would keep him away from the castle during the waking hours so he would not have to suffer the constant temptation that had become Lady Lily Cantrell.

"Your Grace!"

Finn stopped and turned to see Oliver running toward him, his clothes stuck to his body and his hair slicked tight to his scalp. Only something horrible would send the older man out in this weather.

"What is it?" Finn asked, nerves beginning to prickle along his neck. Had Lily been injured or fallen ill? What if she had a seizure or a fainting spell like Juniper suffered?

"It's Lady Lily, Your Grace."

His heart seemed to stop in his chest as he rushed toward his butler.

"What has happened, is she well?"

"She was well enough when last I saw her, but that was as she left, Your Grace. She is heading for London."

Finn blinked away the rain that streamed down his face as he considered the situation. Perhaps this was good news. To have Lily out of his home ensured he would not do something improper like kiss the lass, or worse.

He'd spent nearly every night since the night of their near kiss, thinking of her, fantasizing of lying with her. Her body wrapped around his, her smiles, her face softened by ecstasy.

He was a danger to both of them. It was safer for him to keep his distance.

But for her to go to London by herself…alone…with no funds…

"Did Mrs. Prichard go with her?"

"That had been the plan, Your Grace, initially but then she said she couldn't take the woman with her."

"She's alone in a carriage bound for London?"

"Nay, Your Grace."

He tilted his head, unsure what his butler was not telling him.

"That is, she is not in a carriage. She left on foot when I didn't bring the carriage around for her. You see, I wasn't certain what you would have me do and she refused to wait until I could check with—"

"How long ago did she leave?" Finn snapped, cutting off his butler. He wasn't angry with Oliver, he was irritated with himself, for he knew well enough he was the reason Lily took on such an asinine plan as to walk to London from Scotland.

"Near an hour, Your Grace. It took some time to find you."

Lily had been out walking in this rain for the last hour? The stubborn woman would catch her death. What was she thinking?

"Gabe, may I borrow your horse?"

"Seeing that it's actually your horse, Your Grace, you may take it without my permission."

Finn slid up into the saddle and took off for the road. She couldn't have gotten very far.

OF COURSE, IT had started to rain harder not long after Lily had reached the road. Glaring up at the gray sky, she could see it had no plans of stopping in the near future. It was just her luck.

It seemed fitting that it would be raining. When her life was already on a clear path of destruction, why wouldn't it also be raining? And perhaps she was near to madness as well for this plan, to walk home to London, was indeed mad. But what other choice did she have?

Yes, her mind presented many other options, all of which had her returning to the castle, changing into dry clothes, and getting some of Mrs. Feather's wonderful tea cakes. But that was not going to happen.

There was no turning back. The duke clearly didn't want her there any longer. He had grown weary of having her in his home. Mayhap after she had cut off their near kiss he realized she would not offer the kind of companionship he wanted and decided to have nothing more to do with her. Except she didn't really think that of Finn. He had been nothing but honorable.

She almost stumbled when she considered the other possibility. That after having been nearly trapped into marriage on multiple occasions, he thought she, too, might be set to compromise him to save the shreds of her reputation.

Did he think her so ruthless as to be like Beatrice? Lily was living in the man's home and until a little over an hour ago, had no plans to leave.

Her stay had been far longer than either of them had expected. Almost a month, and still no word from her brother. Perhaps she should have written to her mother, but the woman was fond of drama and would no doubt make more of the situation than was warranted.

Although Lily was ruined and living with a duke in another country, so perhaps some bit of drama might be expected.

As each day passed with no word, she'd worried over what news would eventually come. Or maybe there would never be a letter returned to her. Perhaps she had been cut so effectively they wouldn't even tell her.

Maybe she had been disowned, but until they looked her in the face and told her so, she would not give up.

She could be facing utter humiliation if she did somehow manage to get to London on foot. But at least she was doing something. She was taking her fate into her own hands.

Her little speech had given her the incentive to pick up her pace when she heard the sound of a horse approaching.

She pulled the hood of her cloak forward to hide her face as she moved farther to the side of the road to allow the rider to pass. Hopefully, without casting mud up on her.

But the horse didn't pass. He fell into step beside her.

"Good day, my lady," the duke said as if it was a normal thing to address her as she walked in the rain.

"Good day, Your Grace. Lovely day for a walk, is it not?" she said rather snappishly. She couldn't help it. She was upset and he was within striking distance.

"I'm to understand you are on your way to London."

"You understand correctly."

"On your own, on foot, with no funds." He hadn't asked a question, so she didn't feel the need to answer. "You are angry at me," he said. Again, it wasn't a question, just a statement of fact, but this time she addressed him because her anger had left her as quickly as it had come on.

"There is no reason for me to be angry at you. You did more than anyone else would have done upon finding me in my unfortunate situation." Those words still seemed inadequate for what had happened. "You do not owe me anything else. It is time for me to be on my way. I relieve you of the responsibility and thank you for your kindness."

When he hopped down from the horse, his boots making a squishing sound in the mud, she knew he was not going to make this easy. He still felt responsible for her, because he was a good man. She would have to make him understand.

"I refuse to be relieved," he said.

"I admire your honor, but please get back on your horse and return to your home."

"I will not. Not without you."

She stopped and turned to look him in the eye. Hopefully seeing her seriousness would allow him to let her go.

"Please do not think this is some dramatic ploy to gain your attention. I am not a silly girl who has need to throw a fit because I am being ignored. I have spent most of my life being ignored, Your Grace, so while I didn't like going weeks without seeing you, it wasn't something I had not encountered before. I am not going off in a snit because I didn't get what I wanted." She'd seen her mother do that many times, and for whatever reason it always seemed to work. As if her father rewarded her poor behavior. This wasn't the same. "It is simply time for me to be on my way."

"And what if your family does not allow you to stay?"

"Then I will find work. I can be a governess, or a music instructor." She hoped. She didn't know much about being a mistress except for the things her mother had said about her father paying for the woman's home and trinkets. It wouldn't be her preference, but it was something she could consider as a last resort to put a roof over her head.

She was done living a passive life. She was going to make decisions and see them through. Stand by her mistakes and rejoice in her triumphs knowing everything from here on out was her choice.

"I wish to hire you," the duke said. For a moment her mind was still thinking of becoming a mistress and thought he wished to employ her as such. But then she thought back to the last thing she'd said out loud. "I will hire you to be a music instructor."

She laughed. "You wish to learn how to play the harp, Your Grace?"

"Nay. Not the harp."

"I know what you are trying to do, and again, I thank you for your concern. But I will be quite all right." She might have been selling it a bit thick, but she had to hope that one day it would be true.

"I was wrong to stay away for so long. I was not punishing you and I had not grown weary of having you in my home. I was… I thought it would be easier."

"Easier?"

"To stay away from you so I wouldn't be tempted to do something improper."

As much as it warmed her to hear such a thing, it changed nothing.

"I understand." And she did understand, for she had felt the same temptation. She was glad he wasn't afraid she planned to trap him, or that he despised her. Still, it didn't matter the reason he had been avoiding her, only that he would rather do manual labor in the rain to be away from her. And it wasn't fair to him.

He came to stand in front of her when she started walking again.

"Lily," he said.

At the sound of her name on his lips, the fight went out of her and she was suddenly exhausted.

"Come home," he said, taking her hand in his ungloved ones. "Please?"

"What if they never respond?" she voiced her biggest fear. "What will I do then?"

"It has not been so long yet, to jump to such conclusions."

She nodded.

"Come, let me get you home. Everyone is worried. We'll see you warm and dry and we'll figure out what to do next. You will not be alone, Lily. I promise."

Still holding her hand, he gave it a steady pull until she managed to move her sodden feet in the direction of his horse. He lifted her up to the saddle first and then swung up behind her.

Caging her in with his arms, he took the reins and turned the horse back toward the castle.

Having him so close, soaking in his warmth, she apologized.

"I'm very sorry."

"Nothing for you to be sorry for."

"It just seems to be taking so long for my brother to respond. I don't wish to overstay my welcome. I imagine I have been overstaying since the day I—"

"Lily, you are welcome to stay as long as it takes to hear back from your family. I'll not turn you out. And I'd rather you stay here where it is safe until we know for certain you'll be received by your family. Besides…" He tilted his head and leaned closer to her ear. "I have missed listening to you play for my entertainment after dinner."

She laughed and shook her head.

"But what if my brother never writes back because he has been forbidden to associate with me?"

"I would think if that were the case, someone would be all too willing to tell you such a thing."

"Maybe," she said. "I'm sorry I made you come out in the rain to get me. I feel rather foolish for thinking I could walk to London."

"I don't doubt you could do whatever you put your mind to. From what I have seen, you are willing to do whatever is necessary. I admire you."

"You admire me? The woman who was duped by a scoundrel and left behind after she was ruined?" She shook her head, but he closed his arms around her and she felt what she thought was his lips against her hair before he spoke.

"You are not ruined, dear Lily. He may have taken your virginity, but that sort of man is not able to ruin someone as strong as you, lass. Hold your head high. You have not been bested by the likes of a ferret-faced weasel of an arse."

He'd made her laugh, which she guessed was what he was aiming for.

"I will not be a victim," she said.

"That's my lass," he answered, and she felt her body tremble at his claiming of her as his lass. She knew he didn't mean it the way she'd thought, but she wasn't willing to shake off the warm feeling his words offered. Not when the rest of her was so cold.

Chapter Fifteen

THE NEXT MORNING when Lily didn't come down to breakfast, Finn worried she'd found a way to leave in the dead of night to take up her journey to London.

Unfortunately, he learned she was not well enough to make the journey down to the breakfast room, let alone into another country.

"The dear thing has come down with a chill," Mrs. MacDougal told him when he asked after Lily.

Finn took the stairs two and three at a time in his hurry to get to her. If she was in need of a doctor, he would send for one straight away. In the dimly lit room, he heard a sniffle followed by a cough. It was not proper at all for him to have entered her room without knocking or being permitted to enter after ensuring she was properly dressed. Hell, even then he shouldn't have been in her room alone.

Where was Mrs. Prichard to push him out of the room to protect Lily?

"Lily?" he said as he went to the window to let in enough light to see.

She was settled against a pile of pillows. Finn imagined Mrs. MacDougal had fluffed each one before placing them for Lily to lean upon.

Lily's hair was down. Brown ripples flowed over her shoulders, obscuring her breasts from his view. She was pale, but not dangerously so, in his opinion. Her cheeks still went rosy at his presence.

"Are you well?"

"Just a bit of sniffles. Mrs. MacDougal insisted I stay in bed this morning so she can fret over me. I feel I upset her yesterday when I left, so I'll allow her fussing today to make amends. It seems only fair."

Finn chuckled, so glad to hear she was not desperately ill. He relaxed and carried a chair over next to the bed.

"You upset me yesterday as well, so I hope you'll brave a bit of fussing from me."

"If I must," she smiled.

"I will allow Mrs. MacDougal to descend on you with her magical broth. In the meantime, I shall retrieve a book from the library to read to you. Do you have a preference?"

"Something with a mystery. I like to try to guess at who is deceiving everyone. I hope to better sharpen my skills so I do not fall prey to such lies ever again."

He shook his head and stood to leave the room. He hated the man even more than he already did for stealing Lily's belief in herself. Wherever the man was this day, Finn hoped he was crippled with guilt. Or something more sinister than guilt.

Spending the day in Lily's room was easier than Finn would have thought. Yes, she was still deliciously tempting, even with a runny nose, but he knew the cost of giving in to his desires. And even more so, the cost of not being strong enough to conquer the temptation. For he had hated not seeing her and spending time with her.

If he had no choice but to test himself with her closeness, he would do it so he would prove himself safe to be with her. He would no longer hide away. All that did was make him want her even more.

He chose a book and read until she drifted off for a rest in the late morning. He returned later when she was awake again. This time, Mrs. Prichard was there, frowning at him for being in the room with Lily when she wasn't dressed for visitors.

In the end, she didn't make him leave when Lily begged the woman to allow him to stay.

"Please, Mrs. Prichard, I'm wearing a robe, and I do feel so much improved when the duke reads to me."

Finn winked at her.

The woman offered a disgruntled "hmm" before falling asleep in the corner. They had won this round.

LILY WAS WELL enough to get out of bed and come down for breakfast three days later. In truth, she had been well enough the day before, but she would admit to no one that she drew out that final day just so Finn would come sit by her bed to see to her amusement.

Along with things she would never admit were her two faked sneezes, a half dozen faked coughs, and wishing Mrs. Prichard would have reason to leave so they could be alone.

That last thing was a foolish fantasy and she was glad for her chaperone's constant vigil, despite her sporadic slumber. Even sleeping, the woman's presence was enough to keep Lily from doing anything improper.

When Finn smiled at her that morning as she stepped into the breakfast room, she was warmed through. All memories of the chill long forgotten.

"It is most wonderful to see you walking about this morning, Lady Lily. Won't you join me?"

"Yes, thank you." She made her way to the sideboard where the footmen helped her fill her plate. But Finn stood and took over for the footman who attempted to help Lily to her seat.

She saw a fleeting glimpse of his dimple as he took in her

heaving plate. But of course, he was too polite to make mention of a lady's considerable appetite.

"I do feel much recovered," she said. "Thank you for your attentions despite it being my own fault I fell to illness." She felt her cheeks heat at her silliness. What he must think of her, knowing all her long list of mistakes since they'd met.

The duke waved off her concern with a flick of his sturdy hand.

"I'm glad you decided to stay." As if that was all he had to say about her blunder. So odd, when she was used to hearing endless warnings and admonishments from her family for the simplest infractions. It was the reason she preferred to stay quietly in the background and not call attention to herself.

Finn chatted easily during their meal, telling her of the improvements he'd made to the far field by assisting with a drainage ditch.

"It was good for me to get out and help with the work. To see what is involved. I've always allowed my steward to oversee such matters. While he does an excellent job, I think it was important for my tenants to see I care about their success."

"An admirable thing, Your Grace. It should be a relationship, shouldn't it?" she asked, thinking of the way her father couldn't be bothered with anyone on their lands. And how shabby some of the cottages were when last she was permitted to go riding near them. "The tenants rely on the castle, but the castle also relies on the tenants. An equal partnership."

He smiled at her and nodded.

"How right you are. Did you learn that from seeing how your father manages his properties?"

Her smile faded slightly as she shook her head.

"No. I'm afraid he has not been a good example of this practice. I read about it in a land management book." She knew him well enough by now not to have bothered hoping that would be the last of that topic.

Which is why she was not surprised when he leaned closer

and asked, "You read books on the subject of land management?"

She pressed her lips together hoping to hold in the explanation, but that lift of his eyebrow practically dared her to share her secrets with him.

"I had been listening in when my father and brother were arguing. The topic was not so interesting so I hadn't noticed when someone came close to the door between my father's study and his drawing room. So, I grabbed up a book so to look as if I'd been reading it." He chuckled, and she went on.

"I was only glad to have picked it up correctly so it wasn't upside down."

He was laughing fully now so she continued.

"Max saw me and was quite displeased. He accused me of eavesdropping—which, of course, I was—so to prove him wrong, I settled in for the next two hours and continued reading the book. In truth, I found it so interesting—far more intriguing than hearing my father berate my brother for spending too much at the gaming tables—I took it to my room that evening to finish it."

Finn was wiping tears from his eyes from laughing so hard. She was happy to have provided some happiness after everything he had done for her.

"Would you feel up for a ride today, so I might show you?"

"That would be lovely. I feel I have been inside for far too long. While I adore the violets in my room, I'd like to see some real flowers today."

Mrs. MacDougal came through with finding a riding habit in June's things. While it was dated, it was in good repair and fit well enough for Lily's needs.

"I hope seeing me in his sister's clothing doesn't cause the duke any pain," Lily said as Mrs. MacDougal helped her dress.

"Nay, lass. I've known him since he was a boy and can say he will only be glad they are put to use. Besides, I doubt the duke notices what ye are wearing when he looks at you."

"Mrs. MacDougal!" Lily's scold lost any real threat when she laughed.

"It is a shame Mrs. Prichard won't be able to join you as she doesn't ride. You two will have to be on your best behavior."

Lily's cheeks went warm at the woman's insinuation. But Lily didn't bother to lie and say she wasn't glad her chaperone could not accompany them. She was looking forward to being with Finn alone.

⁜

Chapter Sixteen

F INN GATHERED UP a bouquet of flowers as they took the longer path through the gardens on the way to the stables. Lily seemed to enjoy being there among the blooms. Mayhap it was simply something inherent to being a woman that drew them to the scent.

Finn shook his head and waited for her to finish inspecting the plants and catch up. While he saw she noticed the flowers in his hand, she didn't ask.

He smiled again, remembering her story of her curiosity catching up with her. She looked lovely in the deep blue riding habit. He had no memory of ever seeing his sister wear it, but assumed it had come from June's room.

He wanted to commission a proper wardrobe for Lily rather than have her use his sister's older gowns, but he knew it would only make Lily feel as if she were more of a bother.

In truth, it would be no bother at all. He rather felt Lily could do with a bit of spoiling. Mayhap a frilly nightgown to replace the maidenly one she'd worn when she'd been sick.

He squeezed his eyes closed to dispel the vision that had arisen when thinking about Lily's nightgowns. Unfortunately the vision wasn't the only thing that had risen. He was uncomfortably hard and his riding breeches didn't leave to hiding such things.

Fortunately he managed before their horses were brought out. After he assisted her up into the saddle, without her needing to use the mounting block, he settled himself on his own horse. His groom handed up the bundle of blossoms he'd gathered.

Before heading out into the field to show her the irrigation improvements, he led them toward the place he'd spent many hours talking to his family.

One-handed, he dismounted and tied his horse to a low-hanging limb. He gave the bouquet to Lily and handed her down. She didn't mistake them as a gift for her, but carried them as she walked next to him toward the spattering of gravestones on the rise of a slight hill.

"It is a beautiful view," she mentioned.

He sniffed. "I'm not sure why cemeteries must be placed in picturesque settings. It's not as if any of them can enjoy it," he grumbled while waving his hand toward the stones marking the final resting places of generations of Lockharts and previous Dukes of Granton.

One day he would be placed here next to the others. And what difference would it make that there was a lovely view as the sun burned off the dew from the thick grass in the valley?

"Perhaps the view is not important for those buried here, but for those who come to visit them. I can see how this view might give someone peace when their heart is hurting."

She was right, of course. That made much more sense. But it caused him to think of who might enjoy this view while coming to visit him here. When he was gone, who would care?

His friends Reese and Shay came to Scotland as often as they could. Would they think to visit him here? Would they share a good bottle of whisky and reminisce on the trouble they'd gotten into as lads?

Would he have a wife or children to mourn him?

He looked to Lily standing there patiently while holding the flowers he'd picked for his mother, and thought of her standing at the front of a church with a bouquet while they married.

Gracious, he was allowing his mind to run wild.

Clearing his throat, he reached out for the flowers, and Lily handed them over. Their fingers brushed and despite both of them wearing gloves, he felt the warmth of the leather covering her hands.

He thought of how warm she would be in other places as well.

Bloody hell.

He was in a cemetery holding flowers for his dead mother and thinking such things. Whatever was wrong with him?

With a sigh, he strode toward the newest stones that marked the graves of the family he'd loved. Still loved and missed every day.

Placing the flowers on his mother's grave, he blew out a quick breath in an effort to rid him of the tightness in his throat.

"Happy birthday, mama," he whispered quietly. But Lily was standing close enough to hear.

"It's her birthday?"

"Actually, it is tomorrow, but my father always started the celebration with flowers the day before. My father used to make such a thing of our birthdays. We were allowed to choose everything that day. From what was served for each meal to what we did."

"What meals did your mother request?"

He smiled, happy she wasn't afraid to ask about his family. Oftentimes, people directed conversations around them, as if he wouldn't want to be reminded of the loss. But it was a relief to speak of his fond memories.

"She would start with Cook's lemon cake for breakfast. Of course, June and I never complained at being able to eat cake for breakfast and in fact, we asked for the same on our own birthdays. For dinner, my mother would ask for rais'd giblet pie, mainly because my father disliked it and we didn't have it often the rest of the year. Blancmange and strawberries for dessert."

"And what did you do on her birthday?"

He pressed his lips together and looked out at the valley, feeling the peace Lily had mentioned. One of his ancestors had done a good thing picking this plot.

"It being May and the gardens burgeoning with flowers, we spent the day digging in the dirt, pulling weeds and planting seeds for new things to grow. We had a very competent gardener, but she liked to do things herself."

"As you have a competent steward?" she reminded him.

He'd not seen the similarity before but was pleased to think he shared something of his mother's personality. Many that remembered Finn's father thought him to be very much like him, from looks to temperament.

But he'd been closer to his mother. And now he thought he might be more like her.

Finn nodded. "Aye. I do like to get dirt on my hands as well."

Clearing his throat, he moved on.

"We had a ball in the evening." He laughed. "Though it was only the four of us so it wasn't much of a ball as it was my mother having a bit too much madeira and dancing around with each of us. At first, we would sing, but later, my father would hire musicians to play as we were horrid at keeping a tune while laughing."

"It sounds wonderful."

"It was. I remember when we were small, how we would stay up late into the evening. Somehow, I would fall asleep watching my parents dancing, and then wake up in my bed the next morning. I guess my father carried me. I'm not sure."

"I imagine they both tucked each of you into your beds. From what you've said they sounded very much in love."

Finn nodded. "Aye. They were. Ruined me for marriage, I think."

"How so?"

"I'll not take a wife who simply wants to be a duchess. Or someone who would make a good wife. I want what my mother and father had. I know it is a rare thing, but I'll not settle for less than that kind of happiness."

She nodded. "I understand. I am of the same mind after seeing how my parents behave with their lovers and mistresses. That is no kind of a marriage I want any part of. Now that I'm ruined, I'm sure I should not be choosy, but I'd rather spend my life alone than be in an unhappy match."

"You are no less deserving of happiness than anyone else. It was a mistake, Lily, but dare I say, having married that lout would have been a much bigger one."

"I agree." Her face scrunched up adorably in distaste.

"Shall we be on our way?" he suggested.

She nodded, but instead of turning to leave, she crouched down to straighten the flowers on his mother's grave and whispered loudly enough for him to hear.

"You raised a fine man, Your Grace."

As if her comment hadn't rattled him, he offered his arm to escort her back to their horses.

They continued on with their ride to the fields where he pointed out the work they had done. She asked informed questions and seemed to impress and befuddle his steward and a few farmers. He felt an unreasonable pride as they left to return to the castle. Lily was not his.

She was simply someone who'd needed his help. Though perhaps they were more. Friends.

He knew he was attracted to her, and was doing his best to keep that under his control. He had spent more than a few nights in his bed with his hand on himself thinking of her and hoping the release would keep him from doing something untoward when he was with her.

She was a beautiful woman, but he would respect her by keeping his hands, if not his thoughts, from being inappropriate at all times.

They shared a quiet dinner and she played two songs for him before saying she was tired and went up to bed, leaving him alone.

He wondered how much longer he would have before the letter arrived that would change everything. She would either leave to return home, something he should be hoping for. Or she would leave to find her own way in the world as a fallen woman. A term he despised for its unfairness.

He hated to think of Lily being rejected by her family, but if that came to be, he would step in to help. He might not be able to offer her a home at *Gealach* for that might be difficult to explain to a wife if he were ever to find one.

But he would see her safe at least. Just as he would for any person he called a friend.

After a restless night with his dreams interrupted by visions of Lily in his bed, Finn rose and dressed to go down to breakfast as he did every morning. But this morning was the first time Lily had arrived before him.

She was fairly beaming when he entered the room, though he saw the worry haunting her eyes as she twisted her fingers where she stood by his chair.

"What is this?" he asked at the same time his gaze fell upon a bouquet of flowers on the table next to a lemon cake. His mother's favorite.

※

Chapter Seventeen

LILY COULD BARELY breathe as she waited for Finn's reaction. It had been a silly thing to do, and perhaps he would hate it. But after hearing of his family's tradition of celebrating birthdays, she couldn't let it pass by without the proper acknowledgement.

If he didn't like this, she could easily ask Cook to change the menu for dinner and dessert so not to make things worse.

"Lemon cake?" he said quietly.

"For breakfast," she noted as if he hadn't realized that already. There was still the normal breakfast fare waiting on the sideboard in case he sent the cake away in disgust, but he smiled at her.

"Thank you," he said quietly, his voice cracking on the last word. She felt his pain even though she had never met his mother and could not feel her loss. But seeing how much he missed his family made her hurt for him.

After helping her sit, he took the knife and cut each of them what could only be called a giant serving of cake. They dug in while exchanging laughter.

"I do feel like I'm doing something naughty by having cake for breakfast," she admitted.

He laughed around a big bite that crumbled off his fork and down his chin.

"Everything is permissible on a birthday, Lady Lily. It's the only way to celebrate."

"Then let us celebrate properly," she said, shoving a forkful of the delicious cake into her mouth.

After their breakfast—if one could call such a gluttony, break-fast—they changed into old clothes then went into the garden to pull weeds and plant the seeds she'd asked Oliver to send for in the village.

"These say they are pink. Let's put them in with the other pink flowers over there," she ordered though it wasn't for her to say. She wouldn't even be there long enough to see them bloom, so why it mattered where they were planted, she didn't know. She only knew that the late duchess had a section of the garden filled with just pink flowers and these new pink flowers should go there as well.

"Yes. Let's put them over there. That is where Mother would have wanted them."

"Was pink her favorite color?"

"Aye. Though she'd tell you she liked all the flowers the same, she had a preference for the pink ones."

"I thought as much. Many of the flowers you picked for her bouquet yesterday were pink."

They toiled away at their task for most of the day, only taking a break for tea and lemonade in the shade when Mrs. MacDougal insisted.

"Her Grace would have been pleased to see ye working among the flowers, Your Grace," the housekeeper said. "It is a lovely thing you did, my lady, to think of such a fine way to remember the duchess."

"It was nothing," Lily said, but Finn shook his head.

"It was not nothing. It's very kind of you."

She accepted his praise, though it hadn't taken much to speak to Mrs. Feather and request a few meals. Still, Lily knew how some of the simplest things meant the most.

The duke didn't seem surprised when the rais'd giblet pie was served for dinner followed by blancmange and strawberries for dessert. But he did stop mid-step as they left the formal dining room and she led him to the ballroom instead of the music room which had become their routine.

"The ballroom?" he asked, pausing again at the door. His eyes went wide when she opened the door and light spilled out into the hallway. Then the music began to play.

"Who…?"

"I hired a few musicians from the village." She smiled and then leaned closer to explain. "You probably wonder how I hired them when I have no money. I promised a few lessons in exchange for their playing this evening so we might have a proper birthday ball. It wouldn't be right to allow Her Grace's birthday to pass without this part of the celebration, now would it?"

He swallowed and she saw the way the light from the elaborate chandelier gleamed in his glistening eyes.

Because the moment was growing too serious, she added, "Unfortunately, if you fall asleep down here, no one will be able to carry you to your bed, Your Grace. I'm afraid I can't manage it, and Oliver declined as well."

He shook his head and then held out his hand.

"Shall we?" he asked.

She gripped his fingers and they began to dance. Mrs. Prichard took an offer of a dance with Nimbly the steward, and Oliver danced with Mrs. MacDougal who had just brought a batch of whisky punch that seemed much too large for such a small gathering. But then Lily remembered they were Scots.

They danced and laughed until well into the night when the punch was all but gone.

"I hope I did not cause you any pain today," she said.

He shook his head, though a little wobbly. "Nay, Lily. It was quite the opposite. I miss her, and when I thought of today as I got out of bed, I did feel that loss. But this… what you did… has been such a joy to remember her and the things she loved. Thank you."

"You're welcome, Finn."

She'd only had two cups of punch, but she blamed the whisky for her lapse in using the man's given name. Why had Mrs. MacDougal added so much whisky? She nearly rolled her eyes at her silly question. The answer was always the same.

They were Scots.

Finn's eyes went wide, the amber and green like flames.

"My apologies, Your Gr—"

"Nay. I liked it. Hearing ye say my name." He blinked slowly, obviously feeling the effects of the punch as well. She noticed his Scottish brogue was more pronounced when he was tipsy.

She stepped back and he stepped forward, stumbling slightly.

It seemed she would need to return the favor of helping him to his bed and removing his shoes. Though his boots looked as if they would prove more cumbersome than her slippers had been. Fortunately, he had a valet to do such things. Although Thomas looked very red-cheeked at the moment.

Leaning on her, Finn allowed her to lead him upstairs to his rooms. Inside, she helped him to the bed where he flopped heavily on a bedspread of dark green.

He offered a lopsided grin, with the dimple, as he reached for her.

"Stay with me, Lily."

The request should have shocked her. Instead she simply looked toward the door to make sure Mrs. Prichard hadn't followed them. But they were alone.

Something that was even more evident when he reached up to run his fingers through her hair, before he pulled her slowly but steadily toward him.

She was not so in her cups this night, so she was able to decide whether she should stop him or go along with his silent request. She almost wished she had consumed more of the punch for then she would have had a good reason for why she didn't stop him.

Their lips touched and she tasted the smokey flavor of the whisky mixed with the fruitiness of the punch. Not surprising the whisky was the more potent of the two.

But she only spared another second on thoughts of punch before she was swept up in the kiss. His tongue entered her mouth in small licks and teases.

She'd only kissed one person until now. And Reggie's tongue had not taunted hers into play, but had lurched in demanding space in her mouth.

She squeezed her lids shut even though her eyes were already closed. She didn't want to think of Reggie when she was kissing Finn. The two were not close enough for comparison. It would be like comparing cats and dogs. No. That was not fair to cats. Damp, ugly garden slugs and dogs.

It took her too long to notice his tongue was gone. In fact, everywhere he'd touched her was gone.

She opened her eyes to see the duke had fallen asleep, his lips still glistening from their kiss. Chuckling, she backed away and put her hand out on the poster of the bed to steady herself.

Glancing down at the duke's feet, she determined she was in no shape to help remove his boots. Not just because they seemed formed to his legs and would take a great deal of strength to remove, but because if she started removing the duke's boots, she might not be able to stop there.

Walking in a meandering trail to the door, she knocked until the door opened and the duke's valet, Thomas, entered weaving a crooked path into the room.

"Finn is in need of assistance," she announced louder than necessary.

At seeing the valet's surprise, she recalled her earlier blunder.

"I mean, Finn's Grace, of course."

"Of course," he said as he pulled the bell. A chamber maid arrived with a look of confusion.

"Please help Lady Lily to her room."

"You must take off my slippers," Lily said with another inappropriate giggle. "Yes, my lady, I shall do that," the maid said.

"I only had two small cups," Lily explained.

"My lord. Two cups for this little thing?" The woman turned back to Thomas. "Is all the house in their cups tonight?"

"Aye, I believe so," Thomas answered with a hiccup. Which made Lily laugh.

"It's a celebration," Lily explained, now whispering quite loudly. "I believe I may be worse than I thought."

"Mrs. Feather's punch sneaks up on ye. Come now, let's get you in order."

I kissed Finn. And it was the best kiss I've ever had. She hoped she only thought that last part rather than said it out loud.

Chapter Eighteen

FINN WOKE FEELING like death had come for him but changed his mind.

If it wouldn't have been for his splitting head he might have laughed at the fact he was in bed but didn't remember leaving the ballroom the night before.

He was sure Lily hadn't carried him.

Lily.

That brought a smile to his face, no amount of pain in his muddled brain could prevent.

They had danced. They'd danced country dances with the others in the house, but then they'd danced a waltz as well.

He remembered the warmth he'd felt when he held her close to him. Until Mrs. Prichard had cleared her throat and flicked her wrinkled fingers at him.

But for those seconds he'd been close to her he'd felt a stirring in his body he'd never felt so intensely before. Her hair had been like silk as his fingers explored the dark locks while they'd kissed. Her tongue had been like fire, burning him to his soul and…

Panic came upon him like a bucket of the icy water pulled from the river when it was engorged with melted snow.

Christ, the river wasn't the only thing engorged at the moment. His cock, usually a randy braggard in the mornings, was painfully hard after recalling that kiss.

No. Not recalling. Imagining. For surely it had not really happened, he'd only dreamed it had. Except his imaginings were not usually so detailed. She'd tasted of whisky punch as he'd pulled her on top of him.

Sitting up too quickly for his aching head, he looked around him to see he was wearing nothing but his shirt. But glory saints, the bed was empty and unrumpled on the other side. Proof he'd slept alone.

Thomas came in then after a soft knock. The man knew he was feeling it this morning then. Likely his valet was not much better.

"How did I get in bed?" he asked the man immediately.

"Lady Lily assisted you, and then I called Annabelle up to help Lady Lily to her bed." If the man were not so professional, Finn was certain he would have looked smug.

"Nothing happened?"

Thomas looked at the ceiling. Hell.

"Something happened."

"I cannot say something happened. I can only speculate and Your Grace does not pay me for speculation."

"Let's say, for the moment, I did pay you for speculation, would you speculate I might have kissed the lady?"

"Given the lady's lips were quite rosy, and her hair rather mussed, I might speculate such a thing happened. Oh, and she did tell us she kissed you. And it was the best kiss she'd ever had."

"That doesn't sound like speculation, Thomas."

"Nay. But I didn't see the kiss myself, Your Grace."

So the kiss had been real then. "But nothing else?"

"Nay, Your Grace."

"Thank you, Thomas."

"Does Your Grace wish for me to send to the kitchen for a restorative?"

"Good God, no. I'll not be able to stomach Mrs. Feather's restorative."

"It may taste like the devil's balls, but it does help."

"I'll take a bath and some strong tea instead."

"Very well."

After a bath and a few sips of tea, Finn dressed and went down to the breakfast room. He had to know if Lily despised him for what he'd done. Had she already fled the castle? Would he go after her if she had or send a carriage to take her the rest of the way?

He found her in the breakfast room, frowning at a cup of foul-looking liquid.

"Give me that," he said, striding over to grab up the cup. At the door that led out to the garden, he stepped out and gave it a good toss, bringing the empty cup inside. He silently apologized to whatever plant would likely die now for having been soaked with the evil liquid.

"But Mrs. Feather said it would cure my head and stomach."

"Only because it will have you retching as soon as it hits your guts. Trust me. 'Tis better to just die." He paused, then stepped back to add, "But tell her it helped immensely. I always do."

"I thank you for sparing me." She hesitated after the sentence as if unsure what to say. In his head he heard her voice say his name. Not his title, but Finn.

Had that happened or did he imagine that as well? Damn whisky stealing his memories and offering a bunch of random fragments in return.

He watched Lily's face turn a deep rose and thought perhaps she had managed more than a bit of fragments. She knew what had happened.

But that meant he'd have to ask.

LILY WORRIED SHE would either be sick or go up in flames there in the breakfast room. And that wasn't taking into account her sour stomach and aching head from drinking two glasses of punch last night.

Two glasses that had wreaked their punishment this morning but had not taken her memories in exchange.

She remembered all too clearly the kiss in the duke's bed chamber. Not just in his bed chamber, but on his bed. Well, she had not exactly been on the bed, she was merely leaning over it. Except no, she'd rested her weight on the duke which meant she hadn't been lying on the bed, but had been lying on the duke... who was lying on the bed. But did that detail matter? She'd gone into his room. And then she'd called for the valet. Thomas knew she had been in the duke's room.

She would be ruined if anyone else found out.

Then she recalled having seen Annabelle. She had been there too. Two people knew she'd been in the duke's chamber. But that didn't mean they knew what had happened. The kiss. There was no way they should assume Lily had done anything more than help the duke to his room before calling for Thomas.

No one would know about this kiss. But before she finished that thought, she recalled whispering a muddled account of how she'd kissed the duke and it was the best kiss. Surely, she hadn't uttered such a confession out loud.

Oh, God. What if she had? She would surely be ruined.

Except...

She breathed a shaky breath and her heart calmed slightly. How had she forgotten such an important piece of information?

She could not be ruined, for she was already ruined.

There was some comfort in knowing one's reputation could not get any worse. Still, she was sure the duke would regret kissing her.

That is if he remembered the kiss, which he most likely didn't.

And if he didn't remember the kiss, he wouldn't have re-membered how she'd called him by his given name rather than his title. She wouldn't go so far as to say her kisses were unforgettable, but she had to think a kiss—from anyone—would be more memorable than a slip of his name.

Very well, then she was sure it would be fine. He didn't remember.

"We kissed," he said matter of factly.

Lily looked longingly at the door where the duke had tossed Mrs. Feather's potion into the bushes. Her death could not come soon enough.

✦ ❦ ✦

Chapter Nineteen

Finn worried Lily might try to escape through the door to the garden as intently as she stared at it. But her feet didn't move to run, so he counted himself lucky.

Why had he been so rude as to just blurt it out like that? What was he thinking? Surely it was better if both of them had forgotten—or pretended to forget—about the kiss and went on as normal.

But he couldn't forget. No. He didn't want to forget.

Lily spared a glance up at him and then shook her head.

"I remember something. I believe it was simply a chaste kiss on the cheek," her eyes were wide and her voice wavered. She was clearly lying and not very well.

"Was it?" he asked. He remembered the touch of her tongue against his. And then there was the matter of her telling his valet they had kissed. Still, if she offered them an escape, he would be cowardly enough to take it.

"Yes," she said, nodding quite emphatically. "In fact, I was going to mention it as well, so no one worried it was more than just an expression of friendship."

"Friendship. Yes. That is what I remember as well."

They shared a look and soon they were grinning at each other. He thought he might tease her about calling him by his

Christian name, but perhaps a less risky topic would be better.

"I believe everyone had an enjoyable evening. I thank you, again, for thinking of it. The celebration was just what we needed. After June died, we've all been rather stuck in mourning."

"I understand. I hope your mother would not have been too scandalized by our attempts."

He chuckled thinking of what his mother would have said if she'd learned of him kissing Lily.

"Is she the one?" she would have asked. Finn would have turned pink under her scrutiny and denied his interest. But that would have been the old Finn, the one that thought all girls besides his sister were to be avoided like peas.

He remembered something his father had told him when he was almost ten and six. "Kissing is better when you do it with someone who matters."

Did Lily matter? Of course, she did. But did she matter in the way his father had inferred? He wasn't certain, but as his head cleared and more of the memory solidified, he knew it had been a damn good kiss.

They were so busy avoiding any topic that could bring them back to discussions of kissing, Finn almost forgot about the post.

Picking up the stack Oliver had left with him, he flipped through until he stopped on one letter in particular. He had to read it twice before deciphering what it said, but there was no mistake. It wasn't for him.

"A letter has arrived for you," he said, thinking his voice sounded steadier than he expected at that moment. He felt as if he were holding his future in his hands. There was only one letter Lily was waiting to arrive. One letter that would come here addressed to her. It had to be—

"It's from my brother. I would know his horrid scribbling anywhere. I'm surprised they could even tell where it was to be delivered."

He and Lily exchanged a steady look before she took a breath and turned back to the letter. Breaking the seal, she opened the message, but stopped before unfolding it. Frowning, she held it out to him. "I can't look. Please read it."

He took the missive she'd practically shoved into his hand.

"Very well." He cleared his throat and began to read, *"Dear Sister, I apologize—"*

"No. Don't read it out loud," she said, while covering her ears.

"But how will you know what it says?" He couldn't help the chuckle that escaped at her reaction.

"You will read it and tell me if it is good news or bad and then I will read it once I know what it says."

He guessed he could understand the logic if one wasn't sure what to expect and didn't want to be caught off guard. With a nod, he turned back to the page and focused on the horrid handwriting so he could make out the words.

Dear Sister,

I apologize for the delay of my response. It is only that Mother fell into one of her spells and went to Bath. Max and I thought you went with her and I expected your letter to be nothing more than a telling of your activities there. Since Bath holds no excitement whatsoever, I hadn't taken the time to open your missive before now.

I spoke to Father of the situation. He thought you were in Bath with Mother as well. But now that he knows you have gone to Scotland to visit a friend, he is requesting you stay there for the duration of the Season, as there is no one here to escort you to any ton functions until Mother returns from her recuperation.

I wish you well, Sister, and look forward to seeing you in a few months.

Your dearest brother,
Matthew

P.S. Max told me not to tell you, but he lost your mare in a game of whist.

He let out a breath and she frowned.

"Is it bad news?" she asked.

Finn rubbed his forehead in confusion. How could a family so easily lose track of one of its members? Especially one he found to be utterly enchanting. So enchanting, he'd kissed her the night before. And not like a bloody friend.

Lily's face had gone pale, no doubt she was expecting the worst, and he was doing nothing to assure her. But in truth he didn't know what to say, so he shrugged and held out the letter before saying, "I'm honestly not sure. They don't seem to be cutting you off."

LILY HAD WATCHED as the duke's amber-green eyes traced back and forth as he'd read the words on the page. His brows had come together, and a crease pinched his forehead. She'd thought he was scowling because he had difficulty reading Matty's terrible handwriting. But when he'd finished, his hands fell to his sides and he'd looked at her blankly, before expressing his confusion.

Lily took the letter and read Matthew's rushed words while wincing. In truth, it wasn't as bad as she'd expected. But it wasn't exactly good either.

She felt her face burn with embarrassment. She wished now she hadn't allowed the duke to read the letter first. How awkward for this wonderful man, who had been nothing but kind to her, to learn that her family hadn't even noticed when she had not returned? They didn't know where she had gone and hadn't cared enough to even read her letter when it first arrived.

Not to mention they wanted her to extend her visit with her "friend."

Not knowing what to say, she shrugged. But it seemed he didn't know what to say either.

"Your family... I—I don't..."

She could hardly bear to stand there as he stammered with what she assumed was anger on her behalf.

"Don't worry. I won't stay on here. Now that I know my mother is in Bath, I will just make my way there."

"Are you worried for your mother?" he asked. "Your brother mentioned a spell."

"No. I'm sure she's fine. It's common for my mother to get upset with my father, and go off on her own. To be honest, I can't actually be sure she is in Bath." Lily didn't want to have to explain how her mother had been known to take up with a lover when Father was not doting on her properly. She would throw a fit and go on her way.

Meanwhile, her father would stay out all night himself when her mother was not in residence. Lily knew he had a mistress, she'd heard her brothers speaking of it. Though when she confronted them Maxwell refused to confirm it, and Matthew said he didn't know for certain. But then he'd winked.

She assumed her father was busy with such endeavors and that was truly the reason why he didn't wish for her to come home. He wouldn't want her to be witness to his debauchery.

Lily had not realized how disreputable her family was until she was facing the duty of having to explain it to a person whose family had been proper in every way.

"Your mother might not be in Bath? She might be... *elsewhere?*" He raised his perfectly arched brow and tilted his head. They shared a silent communication of sorts before she nodded and answered.

"Yes. Elsewhere."

He looked up at the ceiling, the letter he'd taken back from her was now getting crumpled in his hand as his fingers curled up into a fist.

"If you wish to go to Bath to see if your mother is there, I will accompany you. If you would rather stay here until the end of the Season you—"

"I couldn't impose on you, Your Grace." She shook her head. "That is, I can't impose on you any more than I already have." She also thought it might be a good time to take her leave before she had only kissed the man.

If she stayed here, she worried what her wanton body might do next.

"It is no imposition if I am extending an invitation. Or would have extended an invitation if you had not interrupted my attempt." His lip pulled up in a playful smirk.

That smile, with the dimple teasing her, was enough to make her heart pound. She was at risk of giving into her base instincts. She feared the best place for her would be a convent.

"My apologies for my rudeness," she said. "But I have come to know how generous you are in the time we have been acquainted. I thank you for the offer, but I have already over-stayed. I should go."

"Where?"

"Where?" she repeated.

"Where should you go? Your father has asked you to stay away from London and you are not fully certain your mother is in Bath. So where will you go?"

She frowned, for he painted a very bleak picture of her options, indeed. The truth was she didn't know where to go. If she got the whole way to Bath and her mother wasn't there, she wouldn't be able to stay there alone. That was, of course, if she even had a place to stay. She would have to hope she would be given credit on her father's accounts.

"You're biting your lip," Finn mentioned as his gaze studied her mouth intently.

It was a bad habit when she was nervous or unsure of something. While talking about such things with the duke, she was both nervous *and* unsure.

She pressed her lips together so as not to bite them. But also because she still didn't know what she would say in answer to his question.

He let out a sigh and did his best to fold the wrinkled letter before handing it back to her.

"You are not a prisoner here at *Gealach*, Lily. That has never been my intent. I will take you wherever you wish to go, if for no other reason than I don't want you to run off on foot again and become ill. But my sincere hope would be that in the absence of a solid solution, you might consider staying here with me, because I enjoy your company and I don't look forward to staying on at the castle on my own. I would like you to stay." He paused for a moment before adding, "I would surely notice if you were gone."

"You make it sound as if my staying would be a favor to you," she noted with a grin.

He nodded. "Aye. It is. I was restless in London, and I worry I shall be just as restless here if left to my own company."

She studied his face for any sign he was only being polite, but saw nothing but sincerity in his hazel eyes, which were more green than amber at the moment.

She considered what his life would be like if she left. They spent a good part of the day entertaining one another and talking. Who would he debate on endless topics if she left? Imagining him here in this massive castle alone and missing his sister, made her heart hurt for him.

If she were the duke, she would long for someone to speak to, even if it was just a random woman with the worst sort of luck and no amount of good sense.

"To be perfectly honest—and I trust you and I are close enough by this point to be perfectly honest with one another—I would much rather stay here than go to Bath, even if I knew for certain my mother was in residence there. There is not much to do if you have no interest in spending your days floating about in foul-smelling water with a number of foul-tempered women."

"Then you shall stay," he said, making the words sound like both a statement and a question.

"Yes. Thank you, Your Grace, I would like that," she said, thinking she might never want to leave, even when the Season was over and she was invited to come home.

She should have felt a wealth of relief to know her father would allow her to return. Only his disinterest was keeping him from taking her back.

But she felt as if a door was closing. All this time she'd hoped to get this news, well, maybe not exactly this news, but close enough.

Yet, she now found herself wishing the letter had not come. It was silly. The duke would not allow her to stay in his home forever.

But deep in her heart, she did find herself wishing she could stay.

She had one more month here at *Gealach* Castle, before the Season would come to a close and her family would leave London for their home in Cornwall.

One more month with Finn.

Chapter Twenty

ONE MONTH. FINN felt as if he'd gotten a brief stay of execution. He stretched a smile on his face, hoping it looked sincere. Even though he thought her own smile seemed a bit brittle as well.

Did she not want to leave?

He would happily have her stay, but he knew there was only one way to make that happen.

He'd not wanted to marry someone simply to fill the emptiness in his life or to fulfill a duty to his title. He had seen the great love between his parents enough to know he wanted that. And he didn't want to use someone in that way. Now, after his time with Lily, he wanted to think his wish for her to stay was because he enjoyed *her* company. Not just the way she filled his days with something far better than emptiness.

He thought of all the things he liked about Lily, aside from the distraction she provided, and that kiss they'd shared—for he was not supposed to remember that. He loved listening and watching her play any instrument. The way she often closed her eyes as if she were envisioning the music in her mind as another person might read the music from a page.

"I am asking you to stay, your father is asking you to stay. But what do you want to do, Lily?"

She shook her head but he didn't think it was because she didn't know.

"That is just the problem. I cannot trust myself and what I want. For doing what I wanted landed me in Scotland amid scandal and ruin."

He guessed he could understand why she might not trust her own judgement after she'd been shaken so thoroughly.

"I would argue it is not your judgement that caused the error, but that you were at a disadvantage. You didn't have all the necessary information to make a sound choice. I daresay that had The Ferret told you he was indeed a ferret-faced, weasel—"

"Of an arse," Lily supplied when he paused in remembering the litany of foul names quickly enough.

"Aye, him," Finn said before continuing, "If he'd told you he had no true intensions to marry, you would not have spared a moment of your time alone with him."

"No. Never."

"So, you see, your decision-making skills are intact. What you lack is the ability to discern when a man who appears to be a gentleman is lying to you. I happen to be quite adept at it."

"How did you become so adept, Your Grace?"

"I can't speak of such things in front of a lady, but if you were to guess I spent too much time at the gaming tables with my brutish friends while at Heriot's, I would have to admit you are right."

She laughed, which was what he had hoped to do.

"Will you teach me?" she asked.

"Of course. Why don't we stroll the gardens so we might enjoy the day whilst I teach my lesson."

She began to follow him and then stopped.

"Is this part of the lesson?"

He laughed. "No, but you are wise to question my intensions. I am a man after all." He offered a wink before leading her out to the gardens.

After picking her a few blooms, he began sharing what he

knew.

"When a person lies, they generally react in a certain way without even realizing it. Many people cannot hold another person's gaze when they lie to them. They may look away, even if only for a second. Others might fidget. Once you know what it is they do, you can ask a question and then watch to see if the person is telling the truth."

"Do you work for the Home Office, Your Grace?" she asked with a little smile.

"Nay, but I know someone who did and he is better at it than anyone I've ever seen." It was the reason Finn never sat across the table from Reese. It would be more efficient to just empty his pockets and hand it over to the man.

"So how do I know what a person does when they lie."

"You test them."

She tilted her head to the side and narrowed her eyes adorably. She would need to look at him, and he was happy to look at her as well, so he led her over to a bench his mother had placed in a private spot.

He turned to face her and she did the same.

"Now. Ask me three questions. I will answer two questions with the truth and one question will be a lie. Watch for me to react in a certain way when I answer one of the questions."

"What should I ask?"

"Anything you wish to know. If I don't want to answer, I'll simply lie." He offered a wink and enjoyed the flush that touched her cheeks.

"Very well. What month were you born?"

"September." This was true.

"And what date?"

"The fifteenth." This was a lie and while he tried to keep from tilting his head down and to the side, he hadn't succeeded. She must have noticed because she grinned.

She placed her index finger on the edge of her lip as if thinking. He would need to answer the next question with the truth or it would ruin the lesson.

She smiled widely and leaned slightly closer, so that the scent of oranges touched his nose.

"Did you enjoy our kiss?"

Bloody hell. Mayhap this had been a huge mistake.

LILY ALMOST LAUGHED at the look on Finn's face. She'd been able to tell the last answer had been a lie so by his own rules that meant he would tell the truth this time. The opportunity was too good to pass up.

He let out a breath before shaking his head as if realizing how adeptly he'd wiggled himself into a corner. She might have let him off the hook if she didn't want to know the answer so badly.

She'd gone from hoping he hadn't remembered to wanting to do it again in a short amount of time.

"Very well… yes. I did like it. I liked it so much, it hasn't been far from my mind since that night and I think about doing it again more often than I shall confess."

She couldn't help the smug smile that took over her face. She felt like she'd won something of great value.

"I see. So when is your birthdate really?" she all but preened at her success.

"The seventeenth," he said while shaking his head. "It seems your lesson was unnecessary. You are a natural."

She frowned. She didn't know if that was true, for she'd never even considered whether or not Reggie had been telling the truth. She'd wanted it to be true so she hadn't doubted him. She would not be so foolish again.

Fortunately the duke had been easy to read. And even now as she looked at him she could almost tell exactly what he was thinking.

He'd not been lying when he'd said he thought about their

kiss often. She knew he was thinking about it right then. From the way his amber gaze flickered from her eyes down to her lips and back again.

Perhaps it was time for her to reciprocate.

"Should you like to ask me three questions, Your Grace?"

His eyes flared with interest and a slow grin pulled up his perfect lips.

"What month were born?" he asked her the same question she'd asked him.

She went with the truth. "July."

"Hmm… And the date?"

Again, she told the truth. "The twenty-fifth."

She quickly realized this game was not as fun from this side of things.

"Did you like the kiss, Lily?" His voice had dropped low and raspy as his eyes flicked as he watched her so intently.

She had to answer with a lie, which also revealed the truth.

"No," she said, her breath catching on the short word. "I hated every second of it and haven't given it a thought since that evening."

She knew she could have left it with that one simple word, but he had shared more with her and she wanted to be fair.

"Can I kiss you again?" he asked.

She smiled. "I thought there was to be only three questions."

His eyes had gone to a dark gold, all the green seemed to have been eaten up by his large pupils. She leaned closer and nodded her answer before he bent to take her lips.

gave a single nod and turned to walk with him through the gardens once more.

They had escaped catastrophe unscathed this time. He worried how much longer he might protect them both. She would leave to return home in a month.

He hoped he could wait that long.

TWO MORE WEEKS had gone by since the day Lily had kissed Finn in the gardens. They strolled the paths every day and she noticed he always glanced toward the bench where it had happened.

If she hadn't seen the fire in his gaze that day when he told her they needed to stop, she might have thought he hadn't liked the kiss. But she had.

And she'd seen the longing glances he cast her way occasionally, especially when she said something particularly witty. Occasionally she also caught his gaze drop to her lips and his tongue would peek out and touch his bottom lip as if after all this time he could still taste her there.

She knew it wasn't possible for she had done the same thing herself. And while she wished he hadn't stopped them, she was more than glad he had. She realized now just how easy it was to lose oneself in a heated kiss or even a look.

Had she not been kissed into such a muddle by Reggie, she would have liked to think she might have avoided this whole mess. If she'd not been caught up in him she might have seen him for who or what he truly was. A no-good, lying arse.

"You're quiet this morning," Finn said, causing Lily to startle. She'd nearly forgotten he walked beside her that morning as she'd been thinking of that day once again. Not that the duke was forgettable in any way, but her mind had wandered like it always seemed to do when they approached that bench.

The end of the Season was growing near, her father would

expect her to return home in a few weeks. But she didn't want to go. She liked it at *Gealach*. She was safe from rumors here. Or at least it was easy to believe as much. She was residing with an unmarried man with the world's most inattentive chaperone.

She did wonder what was happening back in London. Had Reggie returned? Or had he fallen in a large hole that led to the center of the Earth so no one would have to see him ever again? Unfortunately, she knew her luck was not so good.

If he hadn't fallen in a hole, he would have returned long ago. Had he told anyone what they'd done? Surely that wasn't the kind of thing a man bragged about. Defiling a virgin was grounds for a duel if not just earning one the reputation of a scoundrel. Surely he would have to keep such a secret to hide his crimes.

What would happen when she saw him again at a ball or a musicale? What if he had another woman on his arm? She would have to warn her, but would she listen? And wouldn't her warning serve to condemn her for knowing what he was like? If anyone were to know, she would be ruined.

In truth, she slipped further into ruin every day she stayed in Scotland with Finn. But she couldn't make herself care about that. She only wanted to spend as much time as she could with him.

She felt ridiculous. She'd thought herself in love with Reggie and now she was all but besotted with Finn. Would she spend the rest of her life chasing after men like a lightskirt? Perhaps not, but she couldn't help but notice how she resembled the marriage-minded debutantes who went out of their way to chase down their prey.

She looked up at the man next to her, noting she had not needed to chase him to be graced with his company.

"I wish I didn't have to return to London," she told him the truth. "I know it might seem cowardly to want to hide away here in Scotland rather than face my fate. But I don't care a whit about anything or really anyone in London. I love it here." She let out a breath and when the silence continued, she realized what he might think. "Please don't think I have any designs on staying. I am forever grateful for all you have done for me. And for opening your home to me. It is comforting here. I feel free. I only wished you to know how happy I've been here."

He stopped walking and turned to her, his expression rather serious. She hadn't meant to ruin the lovely day. She wanted to wave off her words, but she knew it was too late for that.

"I like having you here. I will miss you when you leave."

Her heart thrummed in her chest with happiness. He would miss her, as she would miss him. She felt a fool to ever have thought herself in love with that horrid weasel. She saw how one-sided her affections had been.

Now, with this man standing in front of her admitting that he would miss her company, she felt things Reggie had never made her feel. She wouldn't be so foolish to think it changed her circumstances, but there was genuine attraction on both their parts.

Perhaps in a different time they might have met at a ball and they might have fallen in love and had this life. But she'd been hasty and made a mess of everything.

She didn't think he was playing her false, for one he'd taught her how to detect a lie. But he'd not once attempted anything untoward. A few heated looks and a bit of flirting were all he'd offered since that kiss weeks ago.

Except maybe this instant as he took her hand in his and stared into her eyes.

Oh, my. His amber eyes looked like pure gold as he stared at her. Then, before she realized he'd moved, he was closer, his breath warm on her lips.

Her heart raced as she closed the remaining distance and pressed her mouth to his in a sweet kiss. They were standing behind the bench where they'd been sitting last time they'd kissed.

What mystical bloom put off such powerful scent as to cast a spell over them?

The kiss escalated quickly, growing from a soft warmth to a

sizzling heat filled with pure joy and want. But as the kiss grew deeper still and his tongue entered her mouth, exploring her, she began to feel something else. Just on the edges of her desire.

It started with a gentle buzzing in her head while sparks flashed behind her closed eyes. When his lips pulled away from hers, she opened her eyes to look at him but it was still dark.

Odd, she thought to herself, a second before the world spun and she floated away.

Chapter Twenty-Two

FINN CAUGHT LILY before she hit the ground at his feet. He spared only a moment of smugness at the fact that he had made a woman swoon from his kiss. But when Lily did not rouse, even after he patted her cheek, his smugness was replaced by utter terror.

He carried her into the house and placed her gently on the settee in the drawing room while shouting for Oliver and Mrs. MacDougal.

"Oh, dear. What has happened to the lass?" the housekeeper asked as she bustled into the room.

"She's fainted. We were walking in the garden and she collapsed." He wouldn't go into details on exactly what they'd been doing before she'd collapsed.

"Oliver, send for the doctor right away."

"Of course, Your Grace." Oliver scurried from the room as Mrs. MacDougal assured him it wasn't unheard of for a woman to faint on a warm day.

It had been warm, but surely in the shade of the trees, it wouldn't have been so warm to cause this reaction. He studied her closely and saw no evidence of a seizure. She was just lying still and pale on his settee.

"Why don't you step out of the room?" Mrs. MacDougal

suggested.

"I don't want to leave her."

"I thought to loosen her gown and stays so she might be able to breathe more easily."

"Oh. Of course." He reached over and touched her soft cheek, noticing the cool, clammy nature of her skin. Surely this had not been caused by his kiss. Something else was wrong.

He forced himself to leave the room as memories of his sister filtered in. How her illness started with headaches, and dizzy spells. And then moved on to numbness in her hands and feet until she could no longer walk and struggled to paint.

What if the same ailment had inflicted Lily? He couldn't lose her, too.

Except, that he was about to lose her anyway. She would be returning to her family in London soon. They might not deserve to have her, but that was where she belonged. Or should belong.

He couldn't help but think she belonged here with him instead. He'd grown attached these last months. He considered what he might do to entice her to stay with him and could only come up with one way to secure their fates.

The kiss in the garden had given flight to his soul, giving him a feeling similar to the way he felt when she played for him.

He was no green lad. He'd known several women, widows mostly, but none had ever made him feel like he felt when he was with Lily.

But marriage?

Was he truly ready, or was he desperate to keep her there so he wouldn't be lonely? It wouldn't be fair to ask her until he was certain it was for the right reason, not a selfish act. He would not end up being another weasel arse in her life.

He paced by the door to the drawing room, but Mrs. Mac-Dougal didn't come out to give him a report on how Lily faired. He was ready to open the door to check when the front door opened and a footman entered with the doctor.

"Thank you for coming so quickly," Finn said.

"I was already in my coach heading home from another patient when your rider intercepted me. Where's the lass?"

"In there," Finn pointed to the room where he'd taken Lily. The doctor nodded and slipped inside without giving even a peek into the room.

"I'm sure she will be fine," Oliver said. "I'm sure your mind has gone to the worst possible outcome, but she's a healthy lass. The doctor said a wasting disease such as June's was rare. Surely there's no chance a second woman would succumb to such a rare illness in the same house."

Time seemed to stand still as he paced in the hall, waiting for some word on what was wrong with his guest.

Finally, nearly an hour after he went in, the doctor exited the room with his lips pressed into a stiff smile. The kind one might manage when they had bad news to deliver.

"Is she well? What is wrong?"

The doctor held up his hand to halt Finn's frenzy of questions.

"She is very well. Healthy as can be. It is good for the babe if the mother is in good health."

"The babe?" he croaked, but of course, he understood what the doctor was saying.

"She might take to dizzy spells in the early months. Might also encounter some sickness in the mornings. Sour stomach is common."

Finn nodded, unable to speak. He was still reeling with this news.

Lily was with child. The man who had tricked her into going with him to Scotland and left her in ruin, also left her pregnant with his child.

The doctor cleared his throat and leaned closer after checking the hall to make sure they were alone. Oliver had gone to the study to get Finn a dram of whisky to settle his nerves, so the hallway and foyer were empty when the doctor spoke.

"It isn't uncommon for couples to anticipate their vows, but she's getting quite far along, you'll not want to delay much longer."

"I understand," Finn said, though it took a moment for him to truly understand what the doctor was saying. He'd assumed Lily was carrying Finn's child. She was, after all, living with him. And even now, Mrs. Prichard was nowhere to be found. She was likely napping in her room. Who wouldn't jump to such a conclusion that he and Lily planned to wed?

Hadn't he just considered the thought of marrying her so she could stay with him? He enjoyed her company, and thought she cared for him. But now, she *needed* to marry. She needed him.

He nodded to the doctor again, feeling slightly dizzy himself.

"Aye. I think you're right. We will need to move things along."

The doctor gave him a hard pat on the shoulder before turning for the door and leaving the house.

The door opened again and Mrs. MacDougal came out.

"How is she?" Finn asked the woman.

"I can't be sure. She's very quiet, that one. But I can see her thinking and worrying."

"Can I go in?"

"Aye. She's dressed. I shall bring some tea."

"Give us a moment, please, Mrs. MacDougal."

"Ach, aye. Just open the door when you wish for me to bring it in."

"Thank you for seeing to her."

"Of course. She's a precious thing, she is. Reminds me of Junie some. Such a sweet lass."

He smiled, though he didn't think of Lily at all in a sisterly way, so it was difficult for him to see any resemblance. When he'd kissed her that morning, he had wanted much more than a kiss.

As he stepped into the drawing room and closed the door behind him, he began to think of all the things he wanted with this woman, and how he might set things right for both of them. So they might both find happiness. Together.

⟫⟫⟫⟪⟪⟪

LILY HEARD THE door open and close, and then open and close again. She didn't turn her gaze away from the gardens beyond the window. She watched the flowers sway in the breeze. So idyllic, the way they seemed so peaceful, while her life had just been turned upside down.

She recalled thinking her life ruined after that morning she'd awoken in the tavern room to find her betrothed had left her. And then she'd met Finn and found a happiness she'd never known.

She'd thought perhaps her life would not be so bad.

But now…

She didn't know what she would do. Even if she could escape the scandal of running off to Scotland with a man she didn't marry, she would not be able to hide a baby. Her father would not allow her to stay at his home as an unwed mother.

Would he ship her away to a convent? She'd heard the maids at home whispering about such a fate for unmarried girls who found themselves in a compromising situation. She'd listened to their gossip with some confidence she would never find herself needing to know the details.

Yet, here she was ruined even more than she'd thought she already was. Her plan to become a governess, or perhaps a music teacher to support herself was no longer an option. No one would hire her now. And how would she support herself as well as a child?

The silence surrounded her as she watched the flowers sway, but a clearing of a throat dragged her back to the reality she was not yet ready to face.

She turned to find Finn standing in the room, just a few feet from where she sat. How long had he been waiting there in silence?

"Do you know he told me there was no chance I could become with child until we were wed? I didn't think that was right, but I believed him. For what reason would he have to lie about such a thing? And even if it weren't true, it wouldn't have mattered for one day wouldn't make a difference. Would it? It was just one day. Except that one day has made quite a difference. The difference between me going back to my life in London and now having no clue as to what I shall do next."

"Perhaps, you should stay here," he said. Did his kindness know no bounds? She turned in her seat to face him.

"Do you mean it? You would offer employment? I thought to be a governess or a music teacher, but I could learn to cook or clean rooms."

He shook his head. "Nay. I don't wish to offer you employment."

"Oh," Lily said, but it took a few seconds longer for her to realize what he must have meant. She was in unfamiliar waters, but she knew enough about extramarital affairs from the way her mother and father went about. "You wish to keep me on as your mistress?"

"Good God, Lily. Of course not."

"Then I don't understand." She was rather put out though she knew she had no reason to be. Especially not with the duke. None of this was his fault. Her life was in turmoil because of her foolishness. But couldn't the man just say what he planned for her? She couldn't just stay on in his home forever. He would eventually wed and have a family. Where would she go then?

"I don't want you to stay as a cook, or a governess, or a mistress."

"I cannot just stay here. As much as I enjoy the castle and especially your company, I will not be your burden any longer."

"Then perhaps you will be my wife instead. I want you to be my duchess. Will you marry me, Lily?"

For the second time that morning, Lily was in danger of fainting.

✦ ❦ ✦

Chapter Twenty-Three

LILY BLINKED AT Finn and frowned. He worried she would refuse him. He should have considered that might happen. Had he thought she would jump at the chance to be married to him? It was rather arrogant of him to think she would be overjoyed to have another option than the fate that awaited her as an unwed mother.

Most women would need only to hear the word "duchess" before they'd have rushed off to make the arrangements and scrounge up an officiant to see the job done as quickly as possible.

Of course, Lily wouldn't be swayed by a title. She wouldn't even grasp at the opportunity to put her life back to rights after a few missteps.

"I am with child," she finally said as if he wouldn't have been informed on the matter.

It probably should have been her business to share or not to share, but since he'd summoned the doctor, the doctor had told him everything.

"I'm aware."

"It's not yours."

It was his turn to frown. "I took firsts in science at Oxford, so I know well enough how biology works."

"What if I give birth to a son?"

Finn smiled. "I would be overjoyed with a lass or a lad. So long as they are healthy and happy, our lives would be blessed indeed."

"I mean, if I give birth to a son after we are married, he would be the heir to your dukedom."

He let out a breath. Why had he thought this would be an easy thing?

"As a duke, myself, I'm aware how primogeniture works, as well as biology."

"But he wouldn't be your son."

"He would be if you agree to marry me." He was trying to do the right thing. To do what was needed. Why was she making it so difficult?

"But not your blood."

"Yes, as I've already mentioned the stellar accomplishments in biology, I'm aware he or she would not be mine by blood, but there are things more important than blood, Lily. Family, happiness, the life we could have if you say you'll marry me. No one would need to know the child is not mine by blood, for *our* child would be my child in every way that matters."

"What you offer is more than I could ever dream of. It is difficult to resist having all my troubles solved by a few words before a clergyman."

"Actually, I was considering exchanging vows over an anvil so it could be done today."

"Are you certain, Finn?" He remembered that foggy night when she'd called him by his Christian name. She hadn't slipped again. But now he imagined it was warranted since he'd just proposed marriage to this woman for her to use his given name. He found he rather liked hearing his name on her lips. Except it had distracted him from hearing the other words as she'd continued.

"—come to resent me or the baby."

"No one is forcing me to wed you, Lily. I'm asking of my own free will. There would be no resentment as it is what I choose to do." What he didn't know was if she would say yes because she wanted it, wanted *him* or because he was offering a solution to her situation. "I would make sure you never regret it. I would never ask for things or give you any bother, I promise."

It was his turn to frown. He didn't want her to feel beholden to him as if he was the hero in a Theodore Stonecliff novel.

"We have only known each other a few months so it is too soon to ask for anything more than a promise of fidelity. And I will promise you the same. We already have friendship. I think a life of happiness could be built solidly on such a sturdy foundation. Many marriages of the ton don't even have the hope of sharing laughter and interests as we already do."

"It is true it is more than I've seen with my parents and my sisters' marriages."

"Then say yes. Marry me. Today. Put an end to my loneliness. Together we can fill this castle with the laughter of children. You'll not regret saying yes. I'll make sure of it." It was his turn to make promises.

She covered her mouth as tears welled up in her beautiful gray eyes.

"This may be the most selfish thing I'll ever do, but I desperately want everything—the life—you just described. So, yes. Yes, I'll marry you."

He thought his heart might near to burst he was so pleased with her answer. For she'd said she wanted this life with him. It was more than he could have hoped for.

Finn helped Lily down from the carriage in the village. He'd requested his travel coach, not that they had all that far to go, but because it was not adorned with the Granton crest. A number of people stopped to stare at them. Finn had purposefully taken them a few villages away from *Gealach*, so there was less chance they would be noticed.

He smiled down at her and pressed his hand atop hers where she all but clutched onto him. It was unnecessary for he never planned to leave her.

He remembered that evening when he'd seen her sitting

forlornly on the steps of the tavern and the way he'd heard Junie's words in his mind. Now, seeing his bride looking up at him with wide gray eyes, he was so happy he'd stopped.

Looking up at the sky, he winked at his sister for whatever part she'd played in guiding him to this point in his life.

Thank you, Juniper.

⤜⟫⟩✕⟨⟪⤛

LILY HELD TIGHT to the crook of Finn's elbow as he escorted her to the blacksmith's shop.

She'd wanted to wear a fine gown to show him how proud she was to marry him, but he'd insisted on simpler clothing so not to call attention to themselves. Besides, her finest gown had ill-will attached to it, as she had been wearing it the morning her previous groom left her.

She would not think of him this day. He wasn't worthy of taking up any more of her thoughts. She would focus on Finn and his kind offer. He had been her hero that evening he'd brought her to his home, and now...

She paused and he stopped to look down at her.

"I need to say something before we marry," she whispered.

"Very well." He glanced back at the carriage and then to her. Did he think she planned to change her mind? She placed her hand on his and gave it a squeeze, hoping to reassure him.

"I know I have thanked you many times on our journey here today, but I wanted to say that while your offer saved me and my chi—"

"*Our* child," he reminded her.

She nodded.

"Yes." She didn't understand how he so easily claimed this child as his own. Her throat grew tight and she rushed through the words so she wouldn't break down into tears. "I truly think we can be happy, Finn. You are not only saving me from ruin today. I am so very pleased to be your wife. However it came to be."

He nodded. "Then shall we see it done?"

"Yes."

She felt lighter as they arrived at the shop. But they must not have succeeded in looking like common folk, for the blacksmith stared at them wide-eyed when Finn asked the man to perform a marriage.

"Surely, it's not the first marriage you've officiated for the gentry?" Finn asked. Though they were more than gentry. Finn was a duke.

And she was about to become a duchess. She swallowed against a lump that didn't seem to budge. She'd been trained to be a nobleman's wife for as long as she could remember.

Her whole life seemed to be for that one thing. Becoming a gentleman's wife. Running his home, bearing his children, and hosting his events.

She'd always wanted love between herself and the man she married. She could say she loved Finn, but there was at least the foundation, as he'd said. It gave her hope that they could build so much more together.

The blacksmith gave a firm nod and stated his price. Finn released her arm and stepped away with the man as they negotiated something in whispers. Finally the blacksmith nodded and Finn gave the man a hefty pouch.

Once the matter of coin was exchanged, the blacksmith saw to blessing the ring Finn had brought for her finger, and speaking the vows they were told to repeat. Lily didn't falter when some of the words slid into Gaelic. She just did her best to speak them.

"I pronounce ye, husband and wife. Ye may kiss yer lass."

Finn smiled and leaned down to kiss her, but paused when his lips were hovering only an inch or two from hers.

"No fainting this time," he warned.

She laughed and grasped onto his jacket and tugged him the rest of the way to meet him with a fierce kiss. She felt his smile curl against her lips and thought how perfect this wedding was. She would never forget this day, the happiest of her life.

$$\text{———} \cdot \text{———} \; \maltese \; \text{———} \cdot \text{———}$$

Chapter Twenty-Four

W HEN THEY RETURNED home, Mrs. MacDougal and Mrs. Feather had prepared a proper wedding feast. The spirits were passed around but neither Lily nor her new husband partook of a sip.

She knew what had stopped her. After her earlier mishaps, she knew she didn't want to spend her wedding night with her head a muddle. But as the festivities wore down and Finn offered his arm and a warm smile to lead her to his bedchamber, Lily wished she might have had a sip. Just enough to stop the shaking in her legs as she climbed the stairs at his side.

"Is everything well? If you don't wish to—"

"Everything is wonderful. I do wish to," she sounded more certain than she felt. It was silly really. She wasn't even a virgin. She knew what to expect in his bed.

Uncomfortable fullness, followed by a pleasant few minutes until it was over and she was left feeling hungry, but not for food. She didn't even have to worry about the pain for that part had been done away with by a man who hadn't deserved such a gift.

She paused just inside his door and turned to face him when he closed it behind them. He took off his coat and waistcoat so he was just in his shirtsleeves.

"I should say something," she said, though she wasn't certain how to say what she wanted to tell him.

"Go ahead," he encouraged when she said nothing else. He crossed his arms to wait.

"I'm sorry," she finally said.

"There's no need to be sorry. I'll wait until you're ready."

She shook her head, wishing she'd not spoken at all. She was ruining this perfect moment. But it was too late to stop now, so she pushed forward.

"No. I'm sorry I'm not...I can't give you...I'm sorry I'm already...That I'm not a..." This was the hardest thing she'd never actually said.

His brows pinched for a moment before understanding dawned on his beautiful face and he was shaking his head adamantly.

"Lily, I don't care about that. Do I wish that scoundrel hadn't hurt you in that way, yes, and I always will. But you are my wife. And trust me when I tell you, it makes no difference to me so long as you share my bed every night."

She nodded and let out the breath she was holding. She saw nothing in his eyes that made her think he was anything but sincere.

"Shall we start with kissing? We are quite good at that," she said.

He chuckled and nodded before moving close to whisper against her lips.

"We are very good at that."

Their lips touched, and like the times before, a soft kiss soon turned into an all-consuming need. But this time they didn't need to stop. They could continue on. She reached for his cravat and tried to tug it free without pulling away, but the bloody thing wouldn't come free.

With a frustrated huff, she stepped back so she could focus on loosening the knot as he slid aside his braces, and pulled the shirt from his breeches.

He pulled his shirt over his head and she reached out to touch the flat planes of his chest and stomach, but instead he took her hands and turned her so she was facing away from him.

He started loosening her laces, his fingers pulling them through more adeptly than any maid she'd ever had. She briefly wondered how many times he'd done that service for a woman and decided it didn't matter.

He didn't care about what had happened in her past so she would provide him the same grace with his own past.

He spun her again, causing her to laugh before he was kissing her.

She lost track of which articles of clothing came off next, she was only happy when they were both naked and he was laying her back on his bed, his large body coming down over hers.

She expected he would move inside her and her body tightened as she prepared for the invasion, but he only stopped kissing to look down at her.

"What happened?"

She shook her head. "Nothing. I was just getting ready."

He smiled. "Nay, lass. We have all night. I want to spend most of it touching every part of you."

She didn't understand, but she was not going to argue if it meant putting off that part of the ordeal a little longer. She was happy to kiss him. She enjoyed when he kissed her neck and then gasped when he kissed her breasts and sucked the peaks into his mouth. That was quite pleasant.

He didn't stop there, though, he continued down, and down until he settled her legs to the sides and licked her in the place she was expecting something else. But this, was incredible. As he continued, she felt the familiar building of tension in her body as she had before. As if she were climbing but never reached the peak.

Except as he continued, he slid a finger in her body and the combination of the movements on the inside and what he was doing on the outside were enough to shoot her to that place she'd not gotten to before.

She couldn't catch her breath and her body throbbed as if trying to grip his fingers and hold him there. She realized she was making noises and even speaking, but it was just gibberish and his name over and over. Until his entering her stole her breath away.

She was shocked at how easily he slid inside her body despite the size of him being larger than that bumbling oaf she refused to think of. It seemed her body had smoothed the way, as if welcoming the duke.

When he began to move inside of her, she realized the only feelings she had were pleasure. There was no sting, no burning. Just a warm want.

And then that earlier feeling returned yet again. Urging gasps and sounds from her throat as he built her up and pushed her over the edge. Strange that she would find this place twice in so little time when it had remained out of her grasp that night at the inn. She could only account the difference was this man.

And then as she was still enjoying the echoing throbs of their passion, he stopped moving and she felt the hot pulsing inside of her that indicated he had finished. But his release was so much more satisfying after she had completed her climax as well.

A few minutes of silence were broken when she couldn't help from asking, "What was that?"

She thought she might need to elaborate on her question, but her new husband must have understood for he chuckled in a way she could only think of as smug.

FINN HAD NOT wanted his bride to compare their experience to what had transpired with the arse. But knowing she had not been satisfied did bring him a certain degree of pleasure.

She may not have come to his bed chaste—something he cared little about—but at least he was the first man to bring her to climax. That was an even more desirable first in his mind.

"You have not experienced such gratification before."

She was the one to laugh now.

"And don't you look like the cat that got in the cream over that fact?"

"Should I apologize?"

"No. I think you've earned the right to feel superior. You are so, in every way."

His cheeks hurt from his grin.

"I am pleased to have pleased you, duchess."

"My, I didn't think I cared about the title, but when you say it like that it gives me an odd thrill." Her words were proven by a little shiver against him.

"How did I say it?" He hadn't thought he'd said it in any particular way, but he wanted to make sure he said everything in the same fashion if it caused such a reaction.

"I'm not sure. Possessively?" she pondered.

That made sense. "I imagine I do feel possessive, though not in a barbaric way. But you are mine now."

"I would not judge you for being barbaric, you are a Scot, after all," she teased. "And now that I'm a Scot by marriage, I'm feeling rather barbaric myself for if I am yours, that makes you mine as well, does it not?"

He liked a playful, sated, Lily, and hoped to keep her in this state as often as possible.

"Aye, lass. I am yours, and happy to be so."

She laughed, no, giggled. Probably at her bravery and the outcome. He kissed her shoulder and then her neck before reaching up to claim her lips.

"Are you not tired?" she asked.

"Very. But there is much of the night left and I will not waste a moment in sleep."

"We will do it again?" she asked. From her tone, he thought she was hopeful for such a thing. Without the worry of her being sore, they were able to continue.

"I'll need a few moments to recover, but yes. We can start

again with kissing if you wish."

"Oh, yes. I do enjoy kissing you, Your Grace."

He'd been addressed as "Your Grace" since his father passed when he was ten and six, and in all those years, it had never made him shiver with such excitement as when his wife said it in a breathy, desperate voice. It seemed he wouldn't need as long as expected to recover.

※

Chapter Twenty-Five

L ILY HAD NO idea just how many ways a man and woman could come together.

"That was my favorite," she gasped as she fell next to Finn on the bed. When he'd pulled her on top of him, she'd felt foolish having to ask him what she was supposed to do, but her husband was a kind teacher. And she was a very grateful student.

"You said that the last time," her husband chuckled.

That was true. She'd enjoyed the way he'd pulled her up in front of him while they both faced the same direction. She'd also said it after they'd dozed for a few minutes and he'd slid into her while she was lying on her side looking away from him.

She'd also liked when he'd used his mouth on her to bring her to the same heights as his body had, but she didn't know if that should be counted in with the other positions.

"Must I be forced to choose?" she asked with a put-upon sigh that made him laugh.

"Nay, I will give you ample opportunity to try them all out over and over again."

For as many times as they'd fallen asleep only to be awakened by the other's touches, they should have been exhausted, but Lily had never been so full of energy. She was a bit sore but more from muscles that had been put to hard use after years of being ignored.

"Is this what we do then? This is our life? To eat breakfast, stroll the gardens, and spend the night in bed doing this?"

"Are you complaining?" he asked before placing a kiss on her forehead.

"Not at all, I think it is quite perfect, actually."

He let his head fall back to the pillow and let out a sigh of his own.

"Alas, we will have to do other less pleasant things from time to time."

"Like what?"

"Like seeing to our duties at the castle. And writing to one's family."

Her euphoria slipped away slightly when she considered his words. Since she was the only one of the two of them with any family, she was left to assume he'd meant her.

He wasn't wrong. She would have to write to tell them she had married and was now the Duchess of Granton. A small smile pulled up her lips when she imagined her father's surprise. Her sisters would be all a flutter. And her mother…might not care at all depending on how thorough her footman was at keeping her bed warm.

But since she wouldn't be there to see it, she was less enthusiastic about the task.

"I meant you would need to tell your family," he said after she'd been silently thinking for some time.

"I know." She noticed the sad tone of his voice.

"I'm sorry you've no one to tell our joyous news."

"June would have been so happy. And she would have loved you."

Lily was pleased to think so. She would have certainly wanted to be friends with someone who cared so much for Finn.

"Tell me more about her. How much older was she than you?" She often thought the many years between her and her sisters was the reason they were not closer than they were.

"She was four months older than me."

"Four months? But…?" That wasn't possible. Unless…

"My sister was not my mother's child, but she was raised as such. No one would have ever known my mother didn't give birth to Juniper." He explained further. "My father had a mistress before he married my mother, and while he was faithful to my mother all his days, it was a little too late. The mistress died when June was nearly four, and her uncle sent for my father then. I don't remember my life without her. Many people assumed we were twins. Only much later, were we told."

"Was she upset to learn the truth?" Lily asked, wondering about the child she carried.

"If she was, she didn't say as much. She was always my sister."

"This is why you weren't worried about the child I'm carrying. Because you have seen that family is not always of the same blood."

"This child will be adored, Lily. Just like any of the others we are blessed to have."

Tears welled in her eyes, and she knew she was more than in danger of loving this man. If he had not already been her hero, she would have thought him the king of her heart now.

"And you were wrong," he said.

"Well, I don't think I should like to hear that from my husband very often." She blinked away the tears and cleared her tight throat.

"I do have people to tell my joyous news. My best friends, Shay, and Reese."

"You've spoken of them before. Do they live nearby that we could have them visit?"

"Nay. They are both still in London for the remainder of the Season." She wanted to ask more about his friends, but he threw the blankets back and got out of bed. "Come now. We should inform your family of our nuptials and extend an invitation for them to visit us here at *Gealach*."

She sat up in bed and stared at him before looking down at herself. She was not yet showing. At least not in her gowns. When she was bathing, she noticed a firmness in her abdomen that had not been there before.

She wondered why she had not suspected she was with child before swooning. Perhaps she had been in denial of the facts.

Still, she wondered what would happen to her body in the time it would take her family to come to Scotland.

"If you are worried over the timing, I paid the blacksmith handsomely for his forgetfulness in documenting our marriage last month."

"Last—oh, you are quite clever, Your Grace."

"Yes. I think so. I shall enjoy hearing my wife say that often." He winked. "As far as anyone will know, our child will be born a month early. No one will bat an eye."

Our child. He always called the babe theirs as if there was no doubt. She wondered if he might feel differently if the child were born a boy. Surely, he would regret such a situation. She only hoped he wouldn't grow to resent her son if it came to be.

For now, she would take him at his word, and hope for the best. Actually, she had a lot of reason to do so.

"I often feel as if I missed boarding a ship that was destined to sink." But it wasn't only that her life was spared, but that she was set on a completely new course. "When I met you, I thought my life was over, but now, I feel so very lucky to have been left behind." She laughed. "I didn't expect to ever feel such a thing ever again."

"We shall see if you still feel lucky after your family comes to visit."

She rather enjoyed the solitude they had here in Scotland, away from everyone who might judge her. But worse than being exposed to her family's judgement, would be if they didn't bother to come at all.

How embarrassing it would be for her new husband to see how disinterested her family was with her. But perhaps they would come if the invitation was extended by a duchess.

"I will write to them and invite them to come."

"Very well. The duchess's seal has been put in your study on your desk."

"Thank you." She only paused a moment before blurting, "They may not come." It was best to keep his expectations low, so he wouldn't be disappointed.

Except she wasn't only thinking of his disappointment, but her own as well.

"They will come. If for no other reason than to make sure you are not being held captive by a Scottish barbarian."

She nodded, but doubted even that fate would rouse the proper notice from her family. After all, she'd been abandoned in Scotland and no one had bothered to come to her rescue.

That evening she sat at her secretary and carefully wrote to her parents, and sisters. She affixed the seal with a smile at seeing the cheerful "G" with a sprouting of flowers around it.

The former duchess had loved flowers, and Lily imagined her designing such a beautiful insignia as a new bride.

Lily had just finished the final missive when there was a knock at her door.

"Come in," she said.

Finn entered the duchess's study with a devilish smile, and she could only smile back at him in return. She allowed the love she only that morning realized she felt for him rush over her.

Finn had removed his coat and waistcoat. He wore only his shirt, open at the neck. He was so handsome. Her heart pounded.

For a moment she attempted to fight her reaction. But then she remembered she didn't need to. She only hoped Finn knew she wasn't one to fall into bed with every man who paid her the slightest bit of attention. Even if the last two men who did so, ended up in her bed, that habit had come to an end when she spoke her vows.

She thought to tell him what she was thinking, but then thought better of speaking when he came closer and bent low enough, she could easily reach his lips with hers.

"Are you done with your correspondence?"

"Yes. I just finished. But you should know if I had not, I would have paused the activity for you."

He laughed. "That is good to know. Though I will try not to be a complete boor so you never get anything done."

"Shall we retire to our room?" she asked.

He shook his head, the smile even more devious.

"Nay. We've no need to have to go so far when we have doors that shut."

"Oh, my," she whispered before he claimed her lips.

Chapter Twenty-Six

"THEY ARE COMING. All of them," Lily said in surprise as the missive in her hand fell to her lap. It had been over a month since she'd written to her family to tell them their happy news. Finn had all but assumed they weren't going to respond.

Fortunately he had many ways to keep her from worrying about it. They found endless opportunities to steal away to make love. The bench where they'd kissed had been put to better use than just kissing.

They couldn't get enough of each other. Her appetite for him seemed endless. He wondered if it might be because of her condition. He'd heard from married men that a woman in the early months of pregnancy were hungrier than usual. He was happy enough to keep up with her.

"I told you they would come," Finn said, because a husband did not miss a chance to say so when he could.

"It seems they will be here in the next few days."

His smile dropped away when he saw his wife turn pale.

"Should I have not encouraged you to invite them? Do they cause you such distress?"

She shook her head.

"In truth, they never have. I'm just surprised they wish to come all this way. To see me."

"They are your family. Of course, they would want to see you happy." Though he wasn't certain this was true of Lily's family. From the things she'd said, and the way they were in no kind of hurry to bring her back home when she might have needed their assistance and understanding, they were nothing like his family. Or how his family had been.

"Yes," Lily said with a shaky smile. "I'm sure you're right."

As it turned out, he was not right.

MILLICENT AND HER husband, Baron Chanting, were the first to arrive. Lily thought it might be best to start off with the worst of them. The baroness was eight years older than Lily, so it might seem they should be the closest, but the furthest thing was true.

"Lily," her sister said with her gaze on Lily's husband instead of her. If the flare of her eyes were any indication, her sister found the duke impressive. Who wouldn't? He stood over Chanting by nearly a foot and was handsome in a stormy sort of way. She knew how his face, shaven closely that morning, would be growing rough this late in the afternoon. And how that felt along her thighs. She let out a huff. Visitors meant she wouldn't be able to drag Finn to the settee.

Millie's own husband was rather dowdy. He was ten years older than Millicent, and Lily had heard Millie tell Maribel she couldn't wait for him to pass so she could be a widow. They had a small son, so Millie's future was set.

Lily's brother by marriage gave a small bow and nod to her and Finn.

"Congratulations on your marriage. I hope it is a happy one." He couldn't have looked less enthused. Lily refrained from asking the man to take care with his health so as to put a wrench into Millie's plans.

Instead, she smiled and simply said, "Thank you, my lord. We are so pleased you and my sister have come."

Millie was still looking at Finn as one might consider a delectable dish, when he placed his hand on Lily's lower back and escorted her into the house.

"You must tell me how this situation came to be," Millie said as if there was some scandal involved. The fact that there was a scandal involved should not have been relevant.

She and Finn had only just solidified the story for her family.

"We have plenty of time for that. And we should wait until the others arrive so we only have to tell it the one time," Finn suggested.

Lily pressed her lips together to keep from smiling. She wondered if the reason he only wanted to tell it once was to avoid the chance they would deviate. Heaven forbid each member of her family heard a different account.

In the foyer, Oliver waited for instructions.

"Please see the Baron and Baroness to the Jasmine Rooms."

"This way." He led them upstairs followed by a line of footmen carrying more trunks than was warranted for two adults. Lily wondered if her sister planned to leave before Christmas.

Dear God, please let this visit go well.

"ARE YOU SAVING the Rose Room for Maribel as it is her favorite?" Finn asked when they were out of sight.

"I knew Millie wouldn't want to share a room with her husband so the Jasmine rooms will give them space."

Finn nodded and hoped he'd never find himself in the same predicament. Spending his nights next to Lily had quickly become one of his favorite things.

It was only a few minutes before they were back out on the steps awaiting another carriage to come to a stop. Her father and brothers stepped down. Matthew, the youngest, came forward and picked Lily up as if she were a doll before he spun her around.

Finn's heart fairly leaped into his throat. He'd been so careful with her and now this man was tossing his pregnant wife about. Before he managed to reach out to stop him, he set Lily back on her feet. She smiled, seeming in fine health, but he looked for any sign she was hiding her pain.

"I'm fine," she assured him, likely to relieve his worried frown. "This scamp is my younger brother, Matthew. This is Maxwell, and this is my father, Lord Devon."

Finn pressed his lips together when remembering the marquess's name was Marcus. Marcus the Marquess. He found it more amusing than Lily had. He returned their bows.

"Your Grace," Matthew said, but he was looking at Lily with a smirk. It took a moment before she looked up, realizing he was speaking to her. Finn found that amusing as well. "It's so strange to think of you as a duchess. I do believe that will be the last time I call you that." He shook his head in distaste.

"Sister," Max said, avoiding the title completely.

Her father followed suit, with a simple, "Daughter." He looked her over quickly before turning his attention to Finn. "Are we to stand about out in the poor weather?" With that he turned and went into the house.

Finn and Lily exchanged a look of confusion.

"Do you think he called me "daughter" because he's forgotten my name?" she asked with a wince.

"Of course not." Though he couldn't be sure. As they followed the group inside, Finn spared a moment to look out at the clear blue sky.

This visit was sure to be a mistake his wife would remind him of for all his days.

They were brought out to the steps twice more when Maribel and her husband arrived. Followed by Martha.

After giving their guests time to be refreshed in their rooms, they gathered in the drawing room before dinner. The room was full of chatter, the way such rooms should be. Filled with family.

He gave Lily's hand a squeeze and she cleared her throat before speaking.

"It is time to go into dinner. I thought perhaps after dinner we could gather in the music room and I can entertain you by playing," Lily offered after sending him a nervous smile. He'd encouraged her to play for her family, for surely they would be awed by the experience.

"Rather than sitting around, I think we would be better entertained with a game of charades," Maribel said, and Millie quickly agreed.

"Oh, certainly," Lily was quick to change her plans to appease her sisters. Finn wanted to speak up, but his wife sent him a quick shake of her head.

"A game of whist would be fun," Max suggested.

"I believe you've lost everything but your shirt on whist, what else do you have to offer, brother?" Matthew taunted his older brother who winced.

"What is this?" the marquess asked. Max punched Matthew in the arm before turning to face his father.

"It is nothing of note, Father. Matthew exaggerates."

"Not by much," Matthew muttered loud enough for all to hear.

"I don't know why young men insist on gaming and drinking and carousing. Such a waste of time. I hope you don't allow your husband to overspend his fortune." Millie leaned closer and whispered to Lily. "If you can't keep him in your bed, at least you should be allowed to buy nice things."

He expected Lily to stand up to the vile wretch and tell her Finn was a faithful husband. That she needn't worry about where he spent his nights for he was smitten with Lily, but he watched as Lily seemed to shrink right before his eyes.

His brave wife didn't speak up. She just stood there twisting her fingers as her sister continued on.

"Men like the duke will want the attentions of a more alluring woman," Maribel added. Finn noted Martha didn't say anything.

She was not as despicable as the other two, but she didn't defend her younger sister either.

"But I'm sure he'll want an heir, so you will enjoy his company for a while at least. Unless," Millie looked at the jewels at his wife's neck. "Has he given you any extravagant gifts? That's a sure sign he has a mistress already."

Lily placed a shaking hand on the diamond dangling at her throat, a gift he'd given her just the day before, and the sisters laughed as Lily's face went pale.

Finn had seen enough.

He cleared his throat to get everyone's attention and in his most arrogant, ducal tone addressed the evil creatures he'd mistakenly invited into his home.

"I would remind you all, that Lily is my duchess and outranks everyone in this room, with exception of me. As such, she has chosen the entertainment for this evening. I would certainly think the children of a marquess would understand the proper way for a guest to behave. Did your older daughters not have the benefit of being taught such things, my lord? They do you a grave disservice."

The marquess glared at his older daughters and whispered, "Hold your viper tongues."

Finn knew better than to think he'd done such to come to his youngest daughter's defense, it was only because a duke had called out his children's poor conduct that he had acted.

The baroness gave Lily a snide grin before offering a bow so low it could only be called mocking. "I am most looking forward to hearing the duchess play for us. I do hope you've improved so we will not have to watch you stumble over the keys."

"My wife is the most accomplished musician I have ever heard," Finn said and cast the ruthless woman a stern look before sending a bright smile to his wife who looked as if she wanted to escape the room. He would have happily gone with her.

"Shall we?" Lily said before leading them all into the dining room where things were surely bound to get worse.

Chapter Twenty-Seven

L ILY GAVE ANOTHER longing look toward the door before turning back to her plate. She eventually gathered enough courage to look across the table to Finn. She worried she would see utter disappointment in his eyes, for what else could she expect? She turned into a mouse when in the company of her family.

Even after his set down before coming into the dining room, Millie and Maribel continued to bring up stories clearly set on embarrassing Lily in front of her husband. The boys had joined in, because the boys didn't realize how such stories would make her feel. While they were oblivious, her sisters had been diabolical.

Except Martha, who sat there. She didn't add to the stories, but she didn't offer to change the subject.

She'd thought being married would change things. That they would be impressed, or at the very least not as disinterested as they had been. But this was worse. She'd somehow become a target of her sisters' cutting remarks. When she'd usually been able to avoid their attentions, she was pushed into the light by her husband who was practically beaming at her from his seat at the other end of the table.

She blinked and found herself transformed into the Lily who

made her husband laugh and smile. The Lily who made the duke shake and cry out her name in passion. He was looking at her the same way he always did. As if she was his very favorite person.

She didn't understand how it had happened, but as she felt her lips pull up to return his calm encouragement, she squared her shoulders and faced her sisters as a duchess for the first time.

"This topic grows boring," she said with a stern look at them.

Seeing their mouths hang agape caused Lily to smother a smile before turning her gaze back to her husband with a firm nod.

"I agree, Your Grace," Finn said. "If in fact you were a gangly lass in your adolescence—which I can't picture, mind you—you transformed into the loveliest of swans. Whilst others became old crows."

"Thank you, dear husband. You honor me with your generous words."

"As you honor me with your beauty and kindness."

Her sisters fell quiet for the rest of the dinner, the boys took up the silence by talking about the trouble they'd gotten into. The marquess looked at the empty seat across from him where her mother should have sat and clenched his fingers into a fist on the table.

Lily wondered if he was upset with the boys or thinking about her mother. Surely, he couldn't be jealous that she had chosen to stay wherever she was with a lover. Not when he'd spent many a night with his mistress.

When the time came to go to the music room, Lily felt her palms go damp. Perhaps this wasn't the best idea. She knew she would be able to play adequately, but she didn't think her skill would matter. Her sisters would still spit their venom.

She smiled at Finn and he smiled back. Tonight, she would play for him. Just as she did most nights. Because he enjoyed hearing her play. She would ignore all the others, for they were not who mattered to her.

It was odd that all this time she'd felt unworthy because they paid her so little notice. But now that she had a small bit of their attention she realized these people were not worthy of any more of her time.

She sat at the pianoforte and began playing. At first the room continued on in the usual chatter, but soon it fell into silence. By the time she finished, she expected to turn to find the room empty. But instead, she found her family sitting in shock. Except for Finn, of course, who was smiling at her the way he always did when she finished a piece.

"I'll wager you've never heard that piece before. Because she created it herself," he said proudly.

When her sisters were able to close their mouths, their lips all pinched into frowns and sneers, but they didn't hold the power they once had. For Finn was smiling and he was the only person that mattered to her.

"I'M SORRY I ever thought you needed to invite these people to our home," Finn started as soon as they were closed into their room for the night. "They are horrid. How were you spared becoming a wicked shrew like your sisters?"

"Martha is not so bad," she answered.

"Only because the woman barely speaks."

Lily shrugged. "In truth, I didn't realize how horrible they are. It's been some time since we've all been together under the same roof."

"Except you're not all together. Your mother is not here. I can only imagine where she is." Lily had said her mother often went off from the family to seek other entertainments. She hadn't been specific, nor had she needed to.

"I'm sorry," she said, and he turned around so fast she jumped.

"Don't apologize for them, Lily. You are even more amazing

than I realized for having grown up with those people. And you are not at fault for their behavior and certainly not at fault for their being here. That rests solely on my shoulders."

She smiled then and came closer, reaching up to rest her hands on his shoulders. "They are quite fine shoulders. Perhaps you would like me to rub them."

"Perhaps if you're of a mind to rub something, there is another body part I might recommend."

She laughed and then squealed in alarm when he scooped her up into his arms and carried her to the bed. As soon as she got past her fright, she began tugging at his cravat.

She slowed when he kissed her, distracting her from her plan to remove his clothes. It was a shame for he wanted both things. To kiss her and to be freed from his clothes. He'd settle with divesting her of her own clothes first.

Slowly he reached under her skirt to roll down one stocking and then the next, tugging off her slipper with each. He thanked the gods for whomever put women's laces in the back of their gown so he might kiss her while also loosening her stays. It was quite convenient.

He smiled down at her where she laid on their bed in just her shift. He could see through the thin fabric. The deep rose of her nipples, and the thatch of dark hair between her legs. He noticed the small bump between her hip bones and leaned down to press a kiss where their child grew.

"Good evening, Lord Haliday," he said, using the courtesy title his heir would be given. She shook her head as she always did.

"You can't be certain it will be a boy."

"I would be happy with a lass as well. What will we name her?"

"We shall think on it. Later." The last word was said with a saucy raise of her brow which changed his course. He sucked her breasts through the fabric until he grew impatient and raised it up over her head.

Moments later he had shed his clothes and boots and sucked in a breath as he slid home into her warmth. His cock twitched and he took a moment to steady himself before he could begin moving.

In the month they'd been married they'd hardly gone an afternoon without meeting up somewhere in the house to sate their needs.

"Today was the longest day of my life," he said, making her chuckle for only a moment before her laughter changed into a moan of pleasure and he felt her body clamp down on his. He couldn't withstand the call of her body, and he spent a few seconds later.

Falling back on the bed, they lay next to each other looking up at the canopy over their bed.

"We must send them on their way," he said, and then added, "Tomorrow."

"By the end of the week," she countered.

"Very well. But not a day more."

MARIBEL AND MILLIE were in the drawing room when Lily walked in the next morning. She and Finn had missed breakfast with the family, preferring to share a tray in their room so they could be alone a while longer.

The women both looked up before Lily could retrace her footsteps. It was too late for her to back out of the room without their notice. She hoped to avoid whatever poisonous words they might say. Then she remembered what Finn had told her before they'd gone downstairs. "You are a duchess. You don't have to stand for them to treat you badly."

"Have you improved at all in your embroidery, sister?" Maribel asked with a look at Millicent.

"I'm afraid not. Fortunately, the duke does not seem to care that his pillowcases are plain," Lily said with a smile at the memory of Finn's hands clenching the pillows the night before when she'd sat atop him.

"I'm sure the man finds other things to think about while in bed?" Maribel said teasingly while Millicent giggled.

Lily rolled her eyes, which prompted more laughter from her immature sisters.

"The two of you sound like Maxwell and Matthew with your infantile jests," Martha said as she strode into the room.

Lily offered her a smile, a small gesture to thank her sister for coming to her rescue, but Martha merely shook her head and took a seat at the end of the settee next to Millicent.

The three older Cantrell girls had always been close. Maribel, the perfect one. Martha, the quiet one. And Millicent, the entertaining one. All of them were equally beautiful with their fine features, golden locks, and bright blue eyes. Max and Matty had gotten the same coloring. Only Lily had darker hair and eyes.

"When are you due?" Martha asked a few moments later. Maribel and Millie went stock still and Lily sucked in a breath.

"What do you mean?"

"You are with child, yes? I've had six children. I know the looks of it. Your breasts are swollen." Martha nodded in the direction of her chest.

Millie hooted with laughter while Maribel looked appalled.

"Of course, it makes sense now. The duke wouldn't have married someone like you unless he'd gotten you with child," Millie guessed.

She was wrong, but only in that it wasn't the duke who'd gotten her with child. Lily didn't say anything in response, and not just because her mouth was as dry as a desert.

"How far along are you?" Maribel prodded. "Married or not, if this child is born well before it should arrive, there will be a scandal."

Maribel had no idea just how big the scandal would have been. But that had all been avoided because of Finn.

"She's a duchess, there'll be no scandal," Martha reasoned. "And it seems the duke is happy with the match. However it came to be."

It was a pity that Lily felt affection for Martha for such a poor defense of her, but it was better than nothing.

"Maybe for now," Millie snapped, not willing to offer even the slightest compliment. "Soon you will grow big as this castle you live in, and he'll turn to his mistress to keep him warm at night."

Lily looked down at her folded hands. She couldn't argue with Millie's cruel prediction. She didn't know what Finn would do. She didn't know if he had a mistress in London. She knew he'd only married her to save her from scandal and worse.

She had no right to stop him from doing what he wished after the sacrifice he'd made for her.

"Not all men have mistresses," Martha said, not taking her eyes off her needle and thread.

Millie sniffed while Maribel looked about the room with her lips pinched as if she'd just caught a whiff of something foul. "This is not a topic for ladies to discuss. It's improper."

"It's improper because your Milton got his mistress with a babe?"

Maribel gasped before her eyes narrowed on Millie. "Your Edgar has more than a few bastards running about London."

Millie sneered. "I don't care what he does. When he's rutting on his mistress, I can be pleasured properly by a very talented painter."

Maribel's face seemed to be stuck in that pinched expression. "You are not to speak of such things. Mother always said a lady should keep such things to herself. You will cause a scandal."

"I do think if we were to take a sip of wine each time Maribel utters the word 'scandal,' we would be well in our cups in shy of half an hour," Martha said quietly to Lily.

Lily looked toward her sister in surprise. Not just at her suggestion, but that the woman was speaking to her at all.

"I learned early on when you could get the two of them to turn on each other, you were well out of their line of fire."

Lily looked back to her bickering sisters and back to the sister with the smug smile on her lips.

"You're diabolical."

Martha shared a conspirator's grin. "I was the middle child until you and Max came along. I am cunning. I had to be."

Lily chuckled quietly so as not to draw the attention of the others. Martha was right. Maribel and Millicent fought viciously without even noticing Martha or Lily.

"Thank you for coming. I didn't think you would."

"If I hadn't it wouldn't have been because I didn't want to wish you well. Only that I am happiest at home with my husband and children. I know the two of them think me mad for staying in the country. But I don't care about scandals or mistresses or dubious artists. I care only for my family." Martha looked up at her then. "It might be more common to have a marriage like them. Like Mother and Father's unfaithful union. But I hope you know there is something more than that."

Lily nodded. She did realize it. She didn't think she would ever have such a love match. Finn was kind and seemed happy with their marriage, but she didn't think he loved her the way she did him. Even still, she knew she didn't want the life of her mother or Lily's two sisters who had devolved to calling each other names.

"You're a prude!" Millie accused Maribel.

"Better a prude than a whore," Maribel contended.

"Oh, dear. I do believe they will start slapping each other soon enough. Let us escape now."

Setting down the music book Lily was holding, she rose and quietly followed Martha from the room. Outside in the hall, Martha went straight for the stairs.

Lily wasn't sure if she should follow the other woman, but decided it was her home so she could go wherever she wished.

Martha didn't stop until they got to the third floor where the nursery was. Lily saw the way Martha's face lit up when her little ones noticed her and came running.

"Mama! Mama!" She crouched down so she was closer to their height and Lily found herself doing the same. The little angel with blonde curls and crystalline eyes came over to Lily with her thumb in her mouth. At three, she was the youngest of Martha's children.

Lily noticed the other children. Maribel's two daughters and Millie's son stayed back watching the reunion in confusion. Lily was quick to include them in their playtime and Martha nodded in approval.

"You do not think yourself too important to enter the nursery. You will be a good mother, Lily."

"I hope that's true." Lily had spent much of her life feeling unwanted. She would never allow her child to feel that way.

Chapter Twenty-Eight

"**I** HEAR CONGRATULATIONS are in order," Viscount Dunbar said while Baron Addington snickered.

After spending the afternoon with the men, Finn didn't think Lily's sisters quite so awful, for their husbands were far worse.

Finn tilted his head. "For my marriage?"

"No. My wife said Lily is with child."

Finn wondered if Lily had changed her mind about telling her sisters about the bairn. She'd been set against it, but now these men knew.

Finn smiled. "Aye. It is true. We were waiting to announce it, but since you know, I don't mind telling you, I'm quite pleased."

"So long as it's an heir. Then you can get past this whole business of being married," the baron said, earning a nod from the viscount.

Harry Reynolds, Earl of Bennington, just stood there in what Finn thought was his normal stoic countenance. Martha's husband didn't talk much, and Finn was beginning to wonder if the Earl found the other brothers by marriage as tedious as Finn did.

Lily's brothers and father were just as bad. The younger men spoke only of whoring and gaming and their father seemed proud as punch that they were following in his footsteps.

Finn hoped he'd be a better father.

"I'm sorry the marchioness was unable to make it," Finn said, thinking Lily's mother should have been here when the news of her next grandchild was announced.

The marquess frowned and waved off Finn's comment.

"Better she's not. She would just find a way to make it about her," he slurred. He was already deeply in his cups as he tracked one of the maids when she entered with a message for Finn.

Finn opened the folded piece of paper and closed it just as quickly.

"If you'll excuse me," he said, leaving the men to their debauchery.

Climbing the stairs, Finn entered his bed chamber to find Lily there. She offered a strained smile when he entered, and for the first time since the crowd descended on *Gealach* Castle, Finn worried that her family's visit might be too taxing for his wife.

"Are you well?" he asked as he reached to pull her close.

She shook her head, though he felt it rather than saw it.

"Should I call for the doctor?" he was quick to ask.

"No. It's just…" She winced as she looked up at him.

"They are awful," he guessed what she wanted to say but was too polite to put to words. "We won't last the week."

Her eyes went round and then the two of them broke into laughter at the same time. Finn was near to falling to the ground and Lily couldn't wipe the tears from her cheeks fast enough before another eruption took hold. At one point the room fell into silence as they did their best to draw enough air.

"Hideous," she agreed, though it took some time to get the word out.

"Why did we invite them?" he asked.

She shook her head and pointed at him and he knew what she would say as soon as she could.

"I know it was my idea, but you should have stopped me."

Still laughing, she pointed again.

"Yes, you said they were difficult. You didn't say they were utterly despicable."

They laughed until the situation was no longer funny.

"I'm sorry they are so horrible. How do we get rid of them?"

Finn rubbed his forehead and shook his head. He didn't know what could be done except to hide away in their rooms until they left.

"How long do you think before they would become bored and leave?"

She frowned. "So long as you have food and whisky I doubt they will become bored enough to find their leave."

"I could say we have run out of whisky," Finn suggested, but Lily only needed to tilt her head and raise her brows for him to realize why that wouldn't work. "Aye. You're right. No Scot would ever run out of whisky."

Normally men of the ton found Scots beneath them except when it came to drinking.

"Hmm…" Finn said with a smile. "I might have an idea. I need to get to my study without drawing the attention of any member of your family. Except perhaps Harry."

"Martha's husband barely speaks."

"Aye. That's why he's the only one I can tolerate for longer than two minutes time."

"Do you want me to cause a distraction so you can escape to your study?"

Finn looked down at his wife and a smile pulled up on his lips. Now that he was looking at her, he surely wasn't thinking about her family but rather the way the woman was able to distract him.

"Let's not be hasty. We are here, and there's a bed."

He watched her gray eyes go darker with interest and her smile was certainly a reflection of his own.

"I'll lock the door."

TWO DAYS LATER, Lily tiptoed past the drawing room to escape out to the gardens when Oliver opened the door to let in two very loud men.

"Where is he?" one of them said.

"He went and married without inviting us. He must pay for his insolence," the other said with a heavy burr.

Lily might have been worried for her husband, but knew Oliver wouldn't offer such a hearty greeting to anyone who was a true threat to the duke.

"Where have ye lads been hiding? You haven't been to *Geal-ach* in an age. Lord knows it might have helped for His Grace to have had some company."

"Don't blame us. You know how Finn gets. He said he wanted to be alone when being alone was the worst thing he could be."

Oliver turned and saw her. Offering a smile, he turned back to the men.

"Your Grace, might I make known to you Lord Flemming and Lord Breckenridge."

"This is Finn's lass?" Lord Flemming said before letting out a whistle. "You're a lovely bit. Now I know why he didn't want to wait on us to arrive before snatching ye up."

"More like he was afraid we'd steal her away from him."

Lily's eyes must have been wide. She'd never met such loud, boisterous lords before. At least not ones she wasn't related to.

"Ah! You've arrived," Finn said, coming into the foyer from his study where he'd most likely been hiding.

"Aye. We came right away as ye requested. Where's the rest of the guests?"

Finn gave Lord Flemming a hug and a sound pat on the back before turning his affection on Lord Breckenridge.

"You don't have to start straight away. Did you meet Lily?"

"Aye. We've shocked her already," Lord Breckenridge said and sent a saucy wink in her direction.

Lily couldn't help but take a step closer to Finn. She was sure they posed no danger, but it wouldn't hurt to be closer to her husband.

Finn chuckled at her reaction and pointed to Lord Flemming first. "This is Shay. I've known him since we were eleven when he came to Heriot's. Could barely make out a word he said. Still not always sure. And this is Reese. I've known him even longer than Shay. We've been in trouble more than a few times."

"And have the scars to prove it." Reese pointed to a scar that bisected his brow. "Your husband did this to me. I was mere inches from needing a patch."

Before Lily had a chance to say anything, Mrs. MacDougal came rushing into the foyer. They all hugged and greeted each other heartily.

"The boys used to spend time here when we were lads," Finn explained. "Everyone liked my family and being here at *Gealach*. Shay didn't really have family and Reese had too much."

"I see."

She felt as if she'd been caught up in a wave as the men filled the foyer with boisterous laughter. Finn led them to the drawing room where her family lounged about.

Lily thought it went much like letting two wild dogs into the palace. Reese and Shay were loud and only got louder as they were introduced to her family. When her sisters attempted to escape to another room, the men split up.

Lily could tell by Finn's smile he was happy to see his friends, but Lily wondered why he would have invited them now when they already had more people than they wanted in the castle. The Scots were clearly frightening the other guests with their lewd comments and crude manners.

And then the whisky came out.

At half past eleven in the morning.

Finn seemed caught up in the frivolity as well. He laughed loudly and sang even louder. By dinner, her sisters asked for trays to be sent to their rooms. And later as Lily was heading to her chamber, she was stopped by her father.

"This is a mad house. We will be leaving in the morning. I'm not surprised you've no control over what happens under your roof. You were always a timid thing. I'd suggest you find your spine before your child is raised to become a barbarian."

Lily opened her mouth to defend Finn, but found she was too exhausted to bother. As long as her family was leaving, she would find a way to deal with Finn and his friends later.

Truth be told, she found them to be charming, in the way of naughty little boys. It was amusing to see Finn behaving so unlike himself. She liked seeing him smile and laugh. Even if he couldn't carry a tune in two buckets. He needed to have a bit of fun.

Her maid helped her dress for bed and Lily frowned over at the empty place where her husband normally slept. Would he not come to bed?

She'd no sooner thought it before she heard three loud Scots ascending the stairs while singing a bawdy song about a wench and perhaps a swan?

"G'night, gents. I'm into my bed with m'wife," Finn slurred loudly.

"Give'er a kiss for me," Shay said.

"And me!" Reese added. Good lord, they were going to wake everyone in the castle.

"Aye, I will! Three kisses it is!"

The door burst open and Finn stumbled inside, slamming the door behind him. She worried he would fall and hopped out of bed to help him.

Except he stood upright and smiled at her.

"Did you hear the news?" he asked with no hint of slurring.

"News?" she asked, befuddled by his abrupt change from drunkenness to sober as a stone.

"Your family is leaving in the morning."

"Yes. My father told me."

He picked her up and spun her around. He kissed her and she winced in anticipation of the heavy scents of whisky on his breath, but there were none. Not even the subtle smoky flavor from a single drink.

"You're not drunk," she said.

"Nay. Me and the boys haven't had a drop." He frowned. "Though Reese spilled a good bit on himself. A waste of good spirits, that."

"It was all an act," she said, finally fitting all the pieces of the puzzle together.

"Aye. Your family seemed fit to overstay so I decided to send them on their way." He touched her cheek. "That is what you wanted, isn't it? You're not angry?"

"No." She began laughing. "It was perfect."

He smiled back at her. "Good. Because I'll need your assistance with the final act of our play." He pulled off his boots and coat. Then reaching for her, he went for the bed. But instead of lying down, he stood up on the mattress and helped her to her feet as well.

He began jumping as a child would, but the noises he made were most definitely that of an adult. Groans and moans of passion filled the room as the bed bounced loudly against the wall.

Lily was faster to realize what he was doing this time and began giggling.

She did her part by taking his hands and jumping with him. Throwing in an occasional shriek which made her laugh even more.

Finally, their ruse surged into a few last grunts and they flopped down on the bed, bursting into quiet giggles like rowdy children.

"That should certainly do it," she said.

"It will not shock me if they leave in the dead of night. Especially your brothers. I would love to see the looks of disgust on their faces having heard such things from their sister."

Lily laughed again. "It serves them right for speaking of their doings in front of me all those years. They'd ruined more than a few meals."

Lying next to each other, they shared a look and then Finn rolled closer and kissed her slowly. Heat built between them as their tongues met and flirted with one another.

"Now that they've surely covered their ears, I can make you groan for real," he said before kissing her.

The next morning Lily suppressed her wide grin to go downstairs and see her family off. It wouldn't do for them to know how pleased she was. Let them think she was sad to see them leave.

Millicent was the first to say her goodbyes. She looked Lily over with a look Lily could only call dissatisfaction.

"I don't know what he sees in you. All I can say is enjoy him while you can. A man with that kind of passion will soon grow bored."

"Pleasant travels, sister," Lily said with a smug smile that seemed to infuriate the woman even more.

"Well done," Martha said. "Your husband and his friends could always find work on the stage if necessary."

"You know?"

She laughed. "It's something I would have done myself to get rid of them."

"I did enjoy our visit, Martha."

Martha nodded. "I hope to see you again. It would be nice to have a real relationship with my sister."

Lily gave the woman a hug and didn't have to pretend she was sad to see her go.

Maribel was next.

"He may be a duke, but he's no gentleman. I wish you well, Sister. You have made your bed by marrying such a man. Now you must lie in it."

"As I'm sure you heard, we don't just lie in our bed." Lily quite enjoyed making Maribel's lips pinch up with just a few words. She was getting the hang of it.

"You did that on purpose," Finn said as he came to stand beside her.

"I learned from the best."

Whatever Finn might have said next was cut off when Max and Matty came to hug her, while flashing disapproving looks at Finn.

"If you ever need us, Sister, don't hesitate to call," Matty said.

"I'll be fine," she assured him.

"I don't see how, but best wishes on your marriage and the babe."

She hugged her favorite brother then turned toward Max.

"You owe me a mare."

Max winced and punched Matthew before turning back to her looking forlorn. "As soon as Father loosens the purse strings, I'll be able to replace her."

Lily doubted that would happen.

Her father was the last person to leave, stopping to speak to Finn rather than her.

"We never did get to speak about the dowry."

Finn put up a hand.

"It's not necessary. I ask that you put it in an account for Lily to use as she sees fit." Finn smiled at her. "I never want her to find herself without funds."

Lily's heart stuttered at his words. He'd found her at her lowest. With nothing to her name and nowhere to go, and while he'd stepped in and saved her from some horrid fate, he was also providing security for the future.

"Thank you," she said.

Her father grumbled and left.

When the last of the carriages were out of sight, Shay and Reese came down the steps and greeted them. Gone were the loud, boisterous men, though Shay's brogue was still heavy.

"Now, Lily, you will truly get to meet my friends."

Chapter Twenty-Nine

THAT EVENING FINN sat in the music room and watched as Lily played for him and his friends. They were still and quiet as the music flowed around them. Shay wiped a hand over his face, and Finn wondered if he'd been brushing away tears.

Finn had been moved to such emotions more than once when listening to his wife play. She had a talent for building and breaking a person with her gift.

When the piece concluded, Reese jumped to his feet clapping in earnest.

"My God, she can play. Not just as drawing room entertainment, but she could easily fill music halls and theaters in Town."

"Aye. And if she wished to do so, I would have seen her there myself."

Lily smiled and shook her head. "I'm glad you enjoyed it. But Finn is right. I have no aspirations of fame. And in truth, no desire to go back to London anytime soon."

She let her hand rest on her stomach and Finn smiled at the gesture. She'd been doing it more of late and every time he found himself filled with thoughts of their future with their little one—many little ones—over the years.

"Yes, I imagine Finn will want to keep you safely locked away in his castle while you are increasing," Shay said with a grin.

"Good job, laddie. Not just in securing such a lovely bride but getting her with child with haste. I know how much you missed having a family. Now you're set to build your own."

He and Lily shared a look and he saw the slight shake of her head telling him she didn't want to share the truth with their guests. He had no plan to.

He was content for he and Lily to be the only people to know the truth. Even Oliver and Mrs. MacDougal assumed they had married quickly because Finn and Lily had taken advantage of Mrs. Prichard's poor chaperoning skills.

That was all anyone needed to know.

Finn had seen the way his mother had loved Juniper. The way she'd treated her no differently than Finn. And the happiness Juniper brought to their mother. His mother was a good example, showing him how easy it was to love a child no matter their parentage. Blood was not as important as love.

He occasionally saw the doubt and worry in Lily's eyes when they spoke of the child. She had yet to settle on any names, while he constantly provided ideas for both girls and boys.

It seemed Lily was particularly worried the child would be a boy. If so, he would be granted the courtesy title of the Earl of Haliday, until one day when he became the next Duke of Granton.

Finn had no reservations with this. He planned to raise his children with love and honor. Blood didn't ensure a person was honorable. A title didn't promise respectability.

Spending time with the men of Lily's family proved that. Titled louts all of them. Even her brothers were on a path to debauchery.

Finn and Lily's child might be born with the blood of a weasel arse, but any son of Finn's would know better than to ruin a lady and leave her on her own.

"You sang so well yesterday for my family, should we sing?" Lily proposed and started playing one of their bawdy tunes. They laughed and stood around the pianoforte belting out the lyrics like drunken sailors. Finn joined in, catching Lily's eye. He was pleased to see how much she liked his friends.

He'd not thought how important such a thing might be. How lucky he was that he'd found this lovely woman who filled his days. And most recently his heart.

He knew she'd married him for security, but he hoped one day, it might come to be more.

"You picked a good one," Reese said while Shay managed a solo.

"I did," Finn said. Though there had been no picking. She'd fallen into his life and he'd claimed her.

"I forgive you for marrying her without us. I know you were probably worried Shay or I might steal her away from you if you'd invited us before your ring was on her finger."

Finn laughed off such a thing.

"I also understand why you weren't able to keep your hands off of her, therefore making a quick wedding required."

"There was no reason to wait," Finn said vaguely. He laughed at Shay's slaughtered attempt at singing. "He's really quite horrid."

"It's good to see you happy," Reese said.

"It is good to be happy." And it truly was.

The next week Lily admitted to being sad to see the men leave. Finn had been so happy spending time with them. But as they stood on the top step waving goodbye to Shay and Reese, Finn was glad they were alone again.

"I'm glad I won't have to battle for your attention in the evenings."

She looked up in surprise.

"There was no battle, Your Grace. You are by far the better singer."

He was the one to look surprised. "You think I'm a skilled vocalist?" he asked.

"Oh, God, no. I didn't say that. I said you were better than *them*. You're still terrible, but they are absolutely dreadful."

She spun and ran for the stairs.

"I'll get you for that, Your Grace," Finn threatened playfully as he chased her into the house and caught her on the stairs. Sweeping her up into his arms, he carried her up to their bed chamber and only put her down on the bed when she was well and thoroughly kissed.

⟫⟫⟩✕⟨⟪⟪

"YOU WILL MISS them?" Lily asked as they lay there in the quiet that extended out beyond their room. After weeks of entertaining guests, they were alone again in the castle.

"Not as badly as I would if you were not here. I'm so glad to never have to be alone again."

"Yes." She swallowed or tried to. It was nearly impossible with the big lump caught in her throat. She knew he was lonely. He'd told her as much. And now that they were married it meant he'd always have someone with him if he wished it.

She knew he hadn't asked her to marry him out of love. For a marriage of convenience—hers more so than his—she was pleased they had friendship, respect, and passion, if not love.

But she was often reminded of the reason he'd married her. Or perhaps there was more than one reason. The first being to save her from her downfall. The second to keep him from being lonely. The third, she'd just added, to pleasure him in their bed. Though he did reciprocate that pleasure.

Still, it was an arrangement rather than a need to be together.

She recalled her short time with Reggie and things he'd said to her. That she was the only one who'd understood him. That he'd loved her. That he'd found her more beautiful than any other woman because of her smile.

It had all been lies, but the way those lies had made her feel when she'd thought them true was indescribable.

To be someone's chosen one made a person feel special.

Irreplaceable. Cherished. With Finn she felt affection, of course, how could she not when he'd been so kind to her from the very beginning? She felt gratitude for his offer of marriage, saving her and her child from scandal that would have ruined their lives.

She'd given him no reason to doubt his words when he said it truly didn't matter if her son held the title of duke. But it was one thing to say so now when they were caught up in desire and the child was just a concept.

It would be another thing when the babe arrived. She didn't know what might happen then.

Chapter Thirty

February

FINN SELECTED ANOTHER lily—this one pink—and bundled it with the others he'd collected into a messy bouquet. It had been some time since he'd visited the hot house. It had been the place to find his mother and sister during the cold winter months when the gardens had fallen to decay.

Finn's father had built a second one when the first had been overrun with blooming plants. After Finn's mother had died, Juniper spent even more time in here. It was where she was often found painting. He would sit with her and tell her his thoughts on things that were happening in the House of Lords, or with a tenant. He realized now, how she rarely gave her opinion, but instead allowed him to talk through the matter until he'd stumbled upon what to do.

"I miss you," he whispered. How he would like to speak to her now about Lily and all the feelings he didn't know what to do with.

He tied the bunch together with a bit of string and then thought Lily might want a bouquet as well. Not lilies though. While there were no violets growing inside, he collected daisies and a few purple hyacinths.

"You would like her, June," he said after looking about to make sure the gardener wasn't around. "She's bright and funny. You should hear her play." He smiled, thinking of the times they'd spent in the music room. His thoughts went to those other times when he stopped her from playing so he might take her there on the pianoforte.

For obvious reasons, he wouldn't mention that to the memories of his sister. Instead, other words came out. Concerns he hadn't put a voice to or consciously allowed himself to think about. But as the time drew near for the child to be born, he had begun to worry.

"I fear she feels grateful, June. It was easy enough to swoop in and do the right thing. She's said I've saved her life, but I'm no hero. I was selfish to hold onto her the way I did. I'd been so lonely and she needed me. It was wonderful to have someone need me. But I wish it was more."

He shook his head.

"Don't get me wrong, there is much to be happy with having Lily as my wife. It's only that I wish she hadn't agreed to marry me simply because it was the only option that didn't end in scandal. I'll never know if she would have chosen me otherwise."

He let out a sigh.

"I know, I can practically hear you scolding me for not being pleased with the blessings I have. I am. Soon, we will be a family. She is a delightful woman. Someone I would have chosen if I'd met her in a ballroom and had the opportunity to get to know her. But, would she have said yes, if she'd had another choice?"

With a final sigh, he tied a string around the second bundle and headed for the house. He would be happy. He had no reason not to be.

Inside, he found his wife sitting in the drawing room looking out the window with her hand lovingly caressing the large bulge of her belly.

He often found her like this, deep in thought, and he wished he had the courage to ask her what she was thinking. Did she regret marrying him? Did she still think of the man she'd planned to marry? Finn knew she was angry at him for what he'd done, as evident by her endless names for the blighter. But that was no guarantee she didn't also love and miss him.

When she noticed he'd entered the room, she turned, and he watched as her face lit up with happiness. But just as anger didn't prove a lack of love, happiness didn't prove the existence of it either.

"Hello," she said as he leaned down to kiss her. "What are these for?" she asked as he handed over one of the bouquets.

"I was picking a bunch for June's grave and thought my wife should like a bit of color on this very dreary day."

"You are going to take those to the cemetery?" she asked while shifting her legs down from the settee and rubbing her back.

"Aye, it is the anniversary of her death. I'd like to pay a visit."

She turned to look out the window and then back at him.

"Might I go with you? At least for the walk. I can stay back if you wish privacy, I just want to get out of the house a bit."

Finn shook his head.

"Nay, it is too far to walk. And up a hill. There are icy patches about. I'll not have you fall and injure yourself when you are soon to give birth to our child."

She frowned but then brightened again.

"Might we take a wagon, so I wouldn't need to walk? I need some fresh air, Finn. I feel confined in the house."

"I'm not certain, but I think that might be why they call it confinement. You are supposed to stay close to the house when your time comes so you are not caught unprepared."

"If you allow me to go along, I promise not to go into labor." She even held her hands clasped in front of her to sway him with her begging. If she knew how much those big gray eyes destroyed his defenses he would never win another argument.

"I don't think you have control over such things."

"I will hold the baby in until we've returned to the house.

Please, Finn. I am going to go mad if I must sit inside another day."

He looked her over, taking in the roundness of her large stomach and the child snuggled warmly within. Finn was responsible for both of them. Keeping them safe and happy. But what was he to do when the safe thing made her miserable?

"Do you even think you could climb up in the gig?" he asked, earning a chilly glare from her before he winked.

"Please, Finn," she begged. This time with a sultry pout. "When we come back, we will need to warm up."

A woman in her condition should not be so alluring, yet her offer caused his cock to twitch with interest.

"Very well. But you must hold onto me and allow me to help you."

"I'll not let go of you. Ever."

When she smiled at him like that, it was his heart that twitched with interest. He would need to be patient. Loving marriages had begun with worse things than the friendship and attraction he and Lily shared.

She was his wife. They had all their lives together.

BUNDLED UP IN her warmest cloak, Lily breathed in the cold February air as she stepped outside the house for the first time in more than a month.

It was a horribly gray day for an outing, but she couldn't sit by the window any longer, thinking. Her thoughts had the habit of turning even gloomier than the weather outside.

As the baby's arrival came closer, Lily often found herself worrying about all manner of things. Would she be a good mother?

She was certain that was a common concern for most mothers at this point in their confinement, but Lily had other concerns as well.

Would her child favor Reggie with his blond hair and dark eyes? Lily had had blond hair as a child so it wouldn't be questioned if her child was fair, but the eyes might give them away. Reggie's eyes were dark as a moonless night. Dark as his soul.

Thoughts of what her child might look like often transformed into worry over what Finn might think having to look at another man's eyes in the child he planned to call his own.

Would he come to resent their son or daughter? A son that would become his heir?

Lily often found herself bargaining with God that the child be a girl so she could be loved as Juniper had been without any other complications with the dukedom.

Finn had assured her many times that this child would be loved as a Lockhart, blood or no. But once she began down that trail of worry it was difficult to escape.

If that were not enough, she'd become such a burden on him and his household. She grew tired easily and barely made it through dinner without nodding off, making it difficult to play in the evenings. Finn had said he didn't mind, but hadn't her playing been the way she repaid him for his kindness?

Worst of all was that she knew if she voiced any of these concerns to Finn, he might well get angry at her. So she kept them inside where they festered and grew like an insidious weed. Choking out any joy she'd managed to hold onto.

It was why this excursion was so necessary. She needed to get away from these fears that gripped hold of her each day.

It had not been a graceful thing, getting her in the gig, but her dear husband only chuckled the one time.

"Thank you," she said as he drove them up the hill toward the cemetery. She had much to be thankful for, but for now she was thanking him for allowing her to leave the house.

"I'm holding you to your promise," he said.

She patted the bump. "Not today, little one."

She expected to remain in the gig when they arrived at the cemetery, so she was surprised when Finn reached up to help her down. Not only because of his privacy, but the sheer difficulty in getting her back in. Or perhaps he found that amusing.

"You don't wish to be alone?" she asked.

"You well know how much I detest being alone."

Yes. It was the reason he'd offered marriage, so he would have companionship. She scolded herself for thinking such things as her booted feet settled on the crunchy grass.

His arm came firmly around her to offer support as he held the bouquet for his sister in the other hand. He led her to one of the tallest stones in the plot. She knew from past visits that marked the grave of the previous duke. Finn's father, whom he'd loved. Next to him, was Finn's mother and a tiny stone marking the son that died only hours after being born. Another one of Lily's fears reared up.

Finn must have felt her body tense for he held her closer.

"Watch your step," he softly reminded. He must have thought she'd slipped.

She nodded as they came to stop at the stone that marked Juniper's grave.

Lily envied the love Finn had for his sister. For all the siblings Lily possessed, she didn't think any of them would bring flowers to her grave. Lily felt as if she knew the other woman after hearing all the stories Finn had shared with her.

"She would have been a wonderful auntie," Lily said.

Finn smiled and nodded. "She would have spoiled our child to rot," he said without heat.

She'd been thinking of something she wanted to ask him, and decided now was the right time.

"If the child is a girl, I was thinking we should name her Juniper. What do you think?" Lily asked. It was the first time she'd brought up the topic of naming the child. She'd worried what might happen during the birth or after so naming the child seemed a taunt to Fate.

Finn turned to her in surprise. For a moment she couldn't tell if he was angry or upset. Did he wish to save that name for a child of his own blood? But then he smiled as his eyes glistened.

"Are you certain? That would be lovely. Yes. Thank you."

"Unless you'd rather wait," she added when she should have remained silent.

The smile faded from Finn's face replaced by confusion and then irritation.

"Lily, this is *our* child."

"As far as others know, yes, but we know differently and I don't wish to assume anything."

He frowned and shook his head.

"I *don't* know differently. I know this is my child and I will love them just as I will love the rest of the children we are blessed to have."

"Of course. I'm sorry." He'd said as much many times and at some point she needed to believe him.

With a nod, he turned and placed the flowers on his sister's grave.

"I cannot believe it has been two years since she passed. It is as cold and dreary as it had been that day."

"As if the weather were set by your feelings," she said, giving his hand a squeeze.

"Yes. I do feel rather cold and stormy. Though I am thankful I am no longer alone."

He'd often told her how grateful he was for her companionship. It seemed selfish for her to wish he enjoyed *her* company particularly. He had given her so much to be grateful for. A home, the protection of his name, and most of all he was claiming her child as his own.

Her life was so much better than it would have been. She remembered her concerns of ending up in a convent or a brothel.

Still, she wished to have his heart.

For she had come to love him. How could she not? He was all that was honorable and kind. Doing her best to be grateful for what she had, she gave his arm a pat and gasped at the warmth she felt run down her legs.

"Oh."

Finn turned to her, expectantly, but she didn't answer. At least, not with words. Instead, she simply grasped her stomach and looked down.

"Do not tell me it is time. Not when you insisted on coming out all this way and promised everything would be fine. I'll not have my child born in a cemetery, Lily."

"Then we should return home. Now."

"Now."

$$\text{\textendash} \diamond \text{\textemdash} \diamond \text{❁} \diamond \text{\textemdash} \diamond \text{\textendash}$$

Chapter Thirty-One

A S FINN HELPED Lily into the gig, he continued muttering.
"You promised. You said, 'If you allow me to go along, I promise not to go into labor.' But here you are going into labor."

If her first pain had not hit her then she might have laughed at his grumbling. When the pain subsided, she patted his leg.

"And as you so rightly said, I have no real control over the situation, so you were aware my promise was empty."

"I see that now."

He set the horses to motion and then gave the reins another slap when she groaned with the second pain not long after the first.

"Lily? I'm sorry for complaining about breaking your promise, but if you could just hold on until we get back to the castle, I would very much appreciate it."

"I'm not going to promise anything else."

The horses were hurried along again.

Lily wanted to point out that he was about to shake the babe out of her if he didn't slow the horses from bouncing along, but she knew there was nothing that would keep him from making haste to the castle.

"Hold on. We're almost there. Just over this rise and we'll see the castle and then perhaps two minutes longer. You can wait two minutes, can't you?"

"I'm sure I can. I can't say for the babe."

"Just do your best."

"Yes. I'm doing my best."

"That's my lass."

Lily didn't see the castle because her eyes were clenched shut as she tried to breathe through the pain. The child certainly didn't seem to be very impatient now that he or she was set on coming.

A groom must have seen them and come out to meet up with them.

"Is something amiss?" she heard the man ask as he rode beside them.

"Go for the doctor at once. The duchess is in labor."

"Right away."

It seemed to be only two minutes later she heard the sound of wheels on gravel. Finn had been right about how long it would take to get to the castle. But if that had been two minutes she should not be having another pain again so soon.

The horses stopped and Finn hopped down to come around to her side, all the while yelling.

"The bairn is coming. I've sent a rider to the village to get the doctor. Help me get her inside."

"I can walk," she said before another pain grasped hold and she bent over.

Lily was swept up into Finn's arms as Oliver opened the doors and ran ahead up the stairs to her chamber.

As they passed the foyer, Mrs. MacDougal was shouting orders to the maids to bring water to the duchess's chamber. It seemed like everyone in the castle had been called upon to assist. But Lily knew the bulk of the work would fall on her.

Finn settled her into the bed she'd never slept in. It had already been stripped to the sheets. Mrs. MacDougal came into the room and took charge, removing Lily's half boots and letting down her hair to pull it aside into a sturdy braid.

Annabelle arrived and helped to get her out of her gown.

Finn's face had paled as he clenched her hand in his. He no longer looked like the formidable Duke of Granton, but in his frantic amber eyes she saw the young boy who had, one by one, lost everyone he'd loved.

She wanted to reassure him, but another pain, stronger than the others so far, gripped hold of her and she could only manage a loud scream.

"TIME FOR YE to leave, Your Grace. We'll take care of the duchess from here."

"I just need a moment with her. Alone."

Mrs. MacDougal frowned but waved everyone out.

Finn sat on the edge of the bed and took Lily's hand. She looked up at him, her smile shaky.

He wondered if his own father had felt this same level of panic and fear when Finn's mother was delivering. Birthing bairns was a dangerous business.

"I know we've been having some bit of trouble when it comes to promises today, but I'll ask you for one more," he whispered.

"What is it?"

"Don't leave me, Lily. I know these things can go wrong and you'll tell me you've no control over such things. And, of course, I know that. But please promise you will be here after."

"I will do my best."

"That's my lass." He kissed her and then bent to kiss the lump of her belly. "Please be kind to your mother, lad. I am excited to meet ye, but let's not rush things, hmm?"

"It could be a lass," she reminded him.

"We shall find out soon enough."

He kissed her and gave her hand a squeeze before turning over the room and her care to the battalion of people who came surging in at Lily's next scream. Thankfully the doctor had been one of them.

Finn looked about the corridor to find he was all alone to wait this out.

If there was something closer to the misery of hell here on earth, Finn didn't know of it and never wanted to learn of it. For standing outside the room where his wife lay screaming in pain was pure torture.

His mind flitted briefly to Lily's father who had done this very thing on five occasions. But then thought a man as callous as the Marquess of Devon had probably made use of the time with his mistress instead of worrying over his wife.

It probably wasn't polite to think such uncharitable things of his child's grandfather, but Finn doubted there was any hope for the man.

Finn wished his own father was here to wait with him. How excited the former duke would have been in anticipation of his grandchild.

Oliver came closer carrying a tray that held a bottle and a glass.

"I thought ye may want to drink to the duchess' good health."

"I hope you brought a glass for yourself as well," Finn said.

The butler winked and pulled a second glass from behind his back.

"I would never let the duchess down," the man said.

After filling both glasses higher than was proper, he held up his glass.

"To the bonny duchess, may her pain be quick and may she bear the fruit of the Granton duchy with ease." The man didn't even wait for Finn to raise his glass before throwing the whisky back.

Finn smiled and raised his own glass. "May my wife win this battle, and she and babe be hale and hearty when it is done." He drank his own whisky.

"I'm sorry, Your Grace, but I can't think of anything worse than this," Oliver said when Lily screamed again. "Surely it would be better to wait on the other side of the castle where you wouldn't be able to hear this."

Finn shook his head.

"My place is here as close to her as I can be. If she can bear to face this pain, I will bear hearing it."

"You care for the lass."

Finn didn't bother to answer. He hoped his actions proved how very much he cared for his wife.

"We all hoped she would stay here. We saw how lonely you'd been after Junie died. When we got word you were returning to Scotland last spring, I believe all of us considered the idea of finding work elsewhere so not to see you and feel your pain. When you arrived with Lady Lily, we were relieved that you'd found someone so you would no longer be alone."

Finn nodded and stared into the depths of his empty glass. Was that what he'd done? Found someone to fill the void in his life? Had he used Lily's situation to keep her with him?

He rested on knowing he'd made her a fine offer and given her a happy life when she otherwise would have faced scandal. But he couldn't avoid the truth. He'd needed her. Maybe even more than she'd needed him.

Oliver returned to his post an hour later, leaving Finn in the hall alone.

Hours later Finn noticed Lily's screams had grown weary. She must be exhausted. He'd noticed the sun had long gone despite having not shown much of itself for the greater part of the day.

Finn looked up at the ceiling thinking his family might be up there looking down at him.

"Any help would be appreciated. Please, help her," he begged.

As if in answer, a loud scream came from the other side of the door at his back. Louder than any before it. Finn worried this was her last effort. He was about to pound on the door and demand to be let in so he might say something to give her the strength to keep fighting. But what were words when she'd been at battle for most of the day.

But then he heard it. A quiet snuffling followed by a louder wail.

Hearing the babe crying brought tears to his eyes. The child had a healthy set of lungs as they continued to shriek their indignation to the world.

Finn reached for the handle and froze. It wasn't that he felt he should wait until he was allowed in. It was his castle and he could do what he wanted. What had stopped him was fear.

He could hear the babe and knew the child was fine. But what of his wife? Had Lily survived the ordeal? Memories of his mother, pale and lifeless in her bed came to him and he took a step back from the door.

He considered taking another and another until he was away, but the door opened and Mrs. MacDougal came out holding a bundle of sheets in her arms. It wasn't until she held out the bundle that Finn realized it wasn't sheets. It was his child.

"You've a son, Your Grace. May I introduce to you, the Earl of Haliday."

"Lily?"

"She did well, she did. They are seeing to her now and you'll be able to go in. Just give them a few minutes to finish things up."

Finn reached out and took the babe who looked up at him with dark blue-gray eyes. Lily's eyes. His tiny head was covered with blond hair that seemed too long for such a small bairn. Finn took in all the other features, seeing his wife in each one.

It wouldn't have mattered. Finn did not know what the other man looked like, and didn't care.

"Hello there, lad. I'm your papa. I'll see that you have a happy life."

"Your Grace, you may come in now."

Finn stepped into the room on wooden legs and took the seat

in the same place on the edge of the bed where he'd extracted Lily's promise.

"How are you?" he asked her.

"I'm well enough. I kept my promise."

"Well, it's about time." He winked at her so she would know he spoke in jest.

She reached for the child and he placed their son in her arms.

Looking about the room, he noticed everyone had left them alone. He took advantage by leaning down and kissing her.

"Thank you for giving us a new Earl of Haliday," he said. "It was a fine title when I held it. I'm happy to give it to him and hope he'll keep it for a very long time."

"I hope so as well."

"He'll need another name," Finn said. "My father's name was William. What do you think of it for him? We could call him Willie until he grows old enough to hate it."

Lily smiled and then a crinkle formed on her brow. He almost knew what she was going to say before she said it.

"Are you disappointed it is a boy? Your heir? Your father's name?"

He shook his head and traced a finger over the infant's tiny bump of a nose.

"Nay, I could not be happier, Lily. We have a son."

Tears rolled down her cheeks as she nodded.

"Yes. We do."

Chapter Thirty-Two

A FTER BREAKFAST, FINN asked Lily to walk with him in the garden. With April upon them, new life was pushing up from the cold earth. Soon the gardens would be full of color and sweet scents. Lily considered how different her life was this spring than last.

Her life here in Scotland was wonderful. She had a doting husband who was the very best father. Each day she thanked her stars for him.

"I'm sure you are aware, the Season has started," Finn said out of the blue. Or it seemed to be out of the blue. From the way he looked away and would not meet her eye, she guessed this was the main reason for his invitation to walk with him.

"And what matter is the Season to us all the way up here?"

"As a duke, I'm expected to attend sessions in the House of Lords."

"But you left early in the Season last year, and I will forever be grateful for it."

"Aye. And I wouldn't bother with it this year either except there is a bill being passed that affects us Scots. Shay and Reese have asked for my support and, of course, I wish to lend my voice with my vote."

"Do you plan to go alone?" she asked, thinking of how much

she would miss him if he planned to leave her behind. Though she couldn't say she had any desire to go to London either.

"I was hoping you would come with me. And Willie, of course, because we won't want to be far from him." He smiled and she saw nothing but sincerity in his eyes.

Finn wanted his family to be with him. She couldn't say no.

"Very well. I shall inform Oliver and Mrs. MacDougal we plan to leave *Gealach*."

He smiled and leaned down to kiss her.

"I think we should attend a few society events while we're in London, so everyone can meet my lovely new duchess."

Lily's excitement dimmed at the idea of being out in society, but she made sure not to show her concerns. It had been nearly a year since her misstep with Reggie. Surely no one would bother to remember she'd vanished last season, let alone mention it.

Everything would be fine.

After all, she was a duchess. Who would speak ill of a duchess?

With all their things packed, and Finn's valet and her lady's maid in the second carriage with the nurse, they were ready to depart. Lily stood holding a sleeping Willie and waited for the duke to come out.

She didn't see his horse brought around, and she knew well enough he hadn't ridden home from London last year for he'd offered her a ride in his carriage on that fateful evening.

Still, she wasn't sure where everyone would be sitting.

Finn came out of the house and slowed as he saw her waiting.

"Is something amiss with the traveling coach?" he asked.

"No. It's only, I wasn't certain where you wanted us. I'd like to stay with Willie, but if he will be a distraction we could ride in the other coach."

He smiled and took Willie from her.

"This is the family coach, Lily. The family rides in it. All of them." He winked and shifted her sleeping son so he could offer his hand to assist her into the conveyance. Once she was settled, he passed Willie to her and climbed in.

"Besides," he said once the carriage was set to motion. "How absurd it would be for one person to ride in this large coach while everyone else crowds into the second one?"

She knew well enough he had ridden alone in this coach when he came from London last May. At least for most of the trip. She had accompanied him for the last portion.

She looked around the carriage and smiled. She'd not had need to ride in it since that night. They'd always used the smaller carriage when going to the village or to dinners at the vicar's home.

"I had no idea how much my life was about to change when I first rode in this coach. It seems strange. I'd thought my life was over. I thought I'd end up in a convent or even a brothel."

"A brothel? Did you even know—ah, yes, your brothers." He shook his head. With a naughty grin he said, "What a waste it would have been for you to be hidden away in a convent."

"I thank you for saving me from either fate. I wouldn't have been happy with either." She looked down at the sleeping babe in her arms and then to her handsome husband. "I am happier than I ever thought to be."

"I wish you would stop thanking me. It's as if I didn't get the best end of the bargain. A family of my own. I'm no longer alone."

For the most part William was an excellent traveler. Mostly because he slept the better part of the way. But when he was awake and fed, he was content to sit on their knee and look out the window.

"Did you know I was blond as a baby?" Lily said as Finn looped a finger in Willie's curls. She didn't know what made her say such a thing. She'd been worried Finn would think Willie's hair color came from his father.

Without looking up, he said, "I was blond until my twelfth summer."

"Oh. That makes sense. It is still a lighter brown with streaks that would probably still be blond if touched by the sun."

"Aye. When I used to run about the hills like a Highlander in the summers, it would go to light."

Lily nodded and looked out the window until Finn's voice drew her attention back to him again.

"It is of no matter if our Willie looks like the man who created him. I am his father."

"Yes, you are."

For now, Willie looked like a baby. Lily didn't spend time looking for specific traits that might have come from Reggie. As Finn said, it didn't matter.

But she did worry what would happen years from now when William grew into a man. That was when boys were want to take after their fathers.

Would anyone notice? Would William ask? If so, what would they tell him?

It was one thing to lie to all of the ton, yet another to lie to their child.

"How old was your sister when she learned her mother, your mother, was not her birth mother?"

He let out a long sigh and stretched his legs.

"She would have been fourteen, I believe."

"Was there a reason they told her?"

"She started to have nightmares. Though I wonder if she'd always had them and just told us what they were about then. She was a horrible sleeper." He shook his head. "At any rate, she remembered being hungry and dirty. She was somewhere with chickens about and she was afraid of them. She said a man would yell at her if she tried to keep the chickens away. That was all she remembered. But my mother and father told her the origin of the dream as a way to help her overcome her nightmares. It seemed June's mother went to stay with her brother for a time when she was sick. He had chickens in the small yard. My father saw them when he found out about June and went to get her."

Willie would have no such memories. His whole life would

be spent with Finn as his father. He'd have no reason to ask. No reason for them to be forced to tell him the truth.

"Are you thinking we should tell Willie the truth some day?" he asked after a bit of silence.

"What are your thoughts on it?"

"I can only think what I would want to know. That is, what would be important. I loved my father. If I'd found out later he wasn't the man who'd sired me, it wouldn't have made a difference for William Lockhart was my father in every way that mattered. If I'm a good father to our William, I would hope he would feel the same. And if that's the case, it wouldn't matter if we told him or not. I will make sure he never has a reason to wish he'd been raised by someone else."

She nodded slowly.

"I agree. He will be loved. There would be no reason for him to know any different than the family he has."

Finn nodded as if the matter was settled, and Lily thought maybe it was.

But there was an unknown still lurking about in London. Reggie Flockton would know the truth as well.

Chapter Thirty-Three

FINN AND LILY passed William back and forth for the long journey. If he'd been older, Finn might have thought he'd made a game out of fussing until he was given over to the other parent for a few moments only to fuss yet again.

But if it were, even he got bored of it eventually. While Lily napped on the opposite bench, Willie had dozed off in Finn's arms. It was one of his favorite things. To watch his son's eyelids flutter as he dreamed.

Finn didn't know what kinds of dreams bairns had. Mayhap the boy dreamed of feeding as it was the thing he did best.

"I dream of your mother's breasts as well. Something we've in common." He chuckled at his own joke. Remembering the way his own father used to have the most absurd sense of humor and possibly amused himself more than others. And now Finn was doing the same without his father ever having taught him such a skill—if it could be called such.

Finn wondered what parts of a person were learned and which were inherited. How would William be like him, and how would he be like the blighter whose seed created the lad?

He knew Lily worried over such things. He guessed she thought of it far more than she let on. He did his best to put her mind at ease. But who would dash away his specters?

In truth, it wasn't so much that he had concerns over William looking or acting like the other man, but rather how to be a good father in general terms. As they'd discussed before, love was the biggest factor. But surely there would be more to it.

Discipline was something he worried over specifically. He and June had gotten into a fair amount of trouble when they were young. And their father often had to reprimand them. But Finn never felt he'd been treated unfairly. He always knew he'd deserved whatever punishment was given.

It was hard to imagine the angel in his arms doing anything wrong. His tiny lips began moving in a sucking motion, leading Finn to believe he'd been right that the lad dreamed of feeding.

"I won't be a perfect father, but I'll always do my best, I promise."

The baby stretched and opened his mouth in a wide yawn showing off his toothless gums. Finn's hand was holding Willie's head and when he reached up, his tiny fingers clamped onto Finn's fingertip.

The lad was growing. His grip was stronger and reached farther around Finn's finger than it had three months ago.

As he settled back into sleep, his fingers loosened and slid along his head.

Finn leaned down to place a kiss on his light hair.

"Sweet dreams, lad."

"I think he dreams of eating," Lily said from the other side of the carriage.

"I thought as much. His lips move as if he's feeding."

"Did you want me to take him?" she asked.

Finn shook his head. "Nay, the two of us are fine together."

Finn hoped that would always be the case.

IF THERE WAS anything more seductive than watching Finn with

William, she didn't know it. She'd known Finn's heart was huge and his generosity was unfathomable. But watching him stroke Willie's tiny nose, she knew Finn cared for her son as if he'd been his.

Lily chastised herself. She needed to stop thinking of William as her son. Finn only ever called him their son. He'd never faltered on claiming William as his own. Why did Lily have such trouble?

Of course, she was pleased to have found such an amazing man who offered his name and home for their protection. And without any hint of blame or regret.

Lily needed to forgive herself for her naïve mistake. And while she still thought of her folly with Reggie to be a mistake, she couldn't regret it completely, for it had brought her not just William but Finn as well.

Her family.

Finally, she was important to someone. Even two someones.

"It seems strange that we cannot see him growing one day to the next, but then all at once you realize how much bigger he is than he'd been when he was first handed to me," Finn said.

He seemed in constant awe of everything Willie did. Had she doubted his ability to love her child as his own? She was glad to have been wrong, for Finn clearly loved William.

"I think if we stared at him long enough, we would have to see it happening," she said. She'd thought the same thing many times.

"Mayhap he grows only while we're asleep."

Lily laughed at that thought.

"We are in Scotland. Perhaps fairies come every night and switch him for a larger version," she suggested with a smile.

Finn shook his head. She expected him to argue the possibilities of fairies, but instead he said, "Actually, we crossed over into England while you were napping."

"I see." She looked out the window as if expecting it to look different somehow. Or perhaps she expected all the members of the ton to be waiting to accuse her of having a light skirt.

But, of course, they wouldn't be lurking here at the border. They would instead be waiting for her in London.

She felt her stomach twist at the thought.

Her face must have shown her unease for Finn reached out and placed his warm hand on her cold one.

"All will be well, Lily. You'll see."

She hoped he was right.

GRANTON HOUSE IS *immense*, Lily thought even though she was no farther inside than the foyer. Peeking into the parlor to her left, she realized she was not wrong.

Not only was the home large, but it was very well decorated with beautiful paintings and fashionable furniture.

"Is there a music room in the house?" she asked.

"Of course. You don't think I would bring you to a home with no instruments, do you? I might as well have forced you to live in Newgate," he said with a grin. "I may have even ordered a new pianoforte as the other one had been here for some time. You will be the first to play it."

Lily smiled up at her doting husband. "Thank you."

He waved it off with a brush of his hand. "I did it for myself as much as you. I can't have you playing for me on a ratty instrument, can I?"

The nurse carried William in. He was awake, his eyes wide.

"What do you think, Lord Haliday?" Finn asked, using their son's title.

William looked at Finn and then held out his hand and leaned toward her husband. Finn gasped as he reached and pulled Willie into his arms.

"Did you see that, Lil? He reached for me." Once again, Finn's happy surprise warmed her heart. "Did you want me?"

Obviously, the baby didn't answer, but Finn looked up at her. "He wanted me to hold him."

"Who wouldn't?" she said, earning a wink from him.

"He must know I have fitted out the nursery with every imaginable thing. Shall we go take a look, sir?"

Lily followed them up to the third floor where a few carved wooden horses sat in greeting. The door opened into a large space.

"Dear Lord, Finn. What did you do?"

"He's an earl, Lily, he can't very well stare at the wall all day. He needs things."

Lily would have argued he didn't need quite so many things, but she knew there was no use. This was one of the ways Finn showed his love. In shelves of books and toys. In the downy soft blankets in the crib and the tiny jesters hanging from the ceiling in jaunty poses that swayed when she touched them.

Two smaller beds sat in alcoves as if awaiting the growing family he hoped to have.

"It is lovely."

"That was my bed." Finn pointed to the bed closest to the window. "And Junie slept over here. Much fun was had in this room. I hope you'll be happy here," he told the baby who seemed to look around, taking it all in with drooping eyes.

"I believe someone is ready to make use of his bed already."

Lily took him and swayed him in her arms as he snuggled close and shut his eyes. It was only a matter of minutes before he was out and tucked into his tiny bed.

Finn gave the jesters a push and wrapped his arm around her as he led her out. "Do you wish to see our bed chamber?"

"If there are no happy jesters hanging from the ceiling, I don't know what point there is," she teased.

"No jesters, but I'll see you don't grow bored when lying in our bed." He leaned down and kissed her neck, right below her ear. It was strange how quickly he could make her body respond.

Only a moment ago she'd thought a nap would be divine

after their travels, but now, sleep was the furthest thing from her mind.

"Show me," she whispered.

He led her down the stairs and to the double doors at the end of the hall. The room was done similar to their room at *Gealach*. The duchess's chamber was through a door, though like in Scotland, she didn't think she'd ever use it.

Not when the duke's bed was so large and inviting.

He swept her up into his arms and carried her to the bed.

"Was that necessary?" she asked.

"You were taking too long." He began shrugging off his coat followed by his waistcoat. When she'd not moved to her own clothing, he tilted his head to the side. "Must I do everything?" His wide smile made her laugh as she worked to loosen her gown.

By then he was already disrobed and helping her with her stays and stockings, having thrown the half boots over his head to thump on the thick carpeted floor.

When she was naked, he slowed down and leaned down to kiss her.

"Welcome to London, Your Grace."

"Why thank you, Your Grace."

$$\text{---}\cdot\text{---}\cdot\!\!\langle\!\langle\!\langle\!\rangle\!\rangle\!\rangle\cdot\text{---}\cdot\text{---}$$

Chapter Thirty-Four

THE NURSE PUSHED the pram next to Lily as she tilted her bonneted head up to allow a bit of sun to warm her face. It was a chilly morning, but the bright sun promised a lovely day.

William was missing it as he'd fallen asleep minutes into their walk in the park.

It was because Lily was looking at her son that she did not first notice the man walking next to her.

She turned thinking perhaps Finn had decided to join them after all, but realized the man was too short to be her husband.

She almost didn't recognize him, despite having once thought she would spend her life looking at his face. His sideburns had grown out into fluffy wings about his face, making him look all the more ridiculous.

"Good day, my lady," Reggie said.

Lily thought to correct his address, but that would require speaking to him. Something she didn't want to do.

Turning to the nurse, he smiled to ask, "Who is this handsome gent?"

"He'd be the Earl of Haliday."

Reggie looked back at Lily with a knowing smirk on his face.

"Is that so? And how old is the earl?"

Lily opened her mouth to tell him it was none of his business, but the nurse took it upon herself to answer.

"He turned three months on the eleventh, my lord."

"I see." The smirk grew wider.

"Would you give us a moment, Sara?" Lily said stiffly.

"Yes, Your Grace," the woman seemed to realize Lily was not pleased with the man, but it had been too late.

"Your Grace?" Reggie questioned as soon as Sara was out of hearing. "So you married yourself a duke? And put a cuckoo egg in his nest?"

She wanted to tell the man he was certainly a cuckoo, but to do so would be to confirm his accusation.

"I surely don't know what you speak of, Mr. Flockton." When he opened his mouth, no doubt to explain, she interrupted. "Please, I don't need an explanation. It would only draw out this discussion and as I don't wish to ever speak to you, that is the opposite of what I wish to do. Good day, and good life to you."

She turned to walk away, but the bounder had the audacity to grasp hold of her arm.

"You think you are better than me now that you married a duke?"

"No. Not at all. I knew I was better than you the moment I learned you ran out on me like a feckless coward. Unhand me, you weasel, this gown is new, and I'd rather not have it sullied by your stench."

His overly charming smile twisted into a cruel snarl. How had she ever thought the man handsome? She could see how rotten he was under the dimples and long lashes. He was nothing but a beautiful serpent. Lily could easily commiserate with Eve for being fooled.

Lily turned away from him, tugging her arm from his grip and hurried to catch up with William and Sara.

It was so Lily's luck to run into the very man she never wanted to see again on her first day in the park. She squared her shoulders and held her head higher as she looked about to see if anyone had witnessed the confrontation.

No one was staring at her or pointing, so she brushed at the wrinkles on her sleeve and walked on feeling stronger for having faced down the monster and walked away unscathed.

Perhaps her fingers trembled slightly as she pushed a strand of hair back into her bonnet, but she'd survived the ordeal. It was over. She never needed to think of Reggie Flocton ever again.

"Is everything all right, Your Grace?" Sara asked, a hint of worry in her eyes.

"Everything is splendid," Lily said.

LILY STEPPED INTO Finn's study and waited by the doorway as if needing a formal invitation to come in.

"Such proper manners here in town, Your Grace," he teased and waved her in. He stood and walked around the large desk to greet her with a proper kiss.

"I didn't know if you would be busy while we were here."

"Too busy for you? Never. In fact, I've been waiting here for short on an hour hoping you'd happen by so I might toss you up on my desk and have my way with you."

Lily spun around and for a moment Finn worried he'd offended her, but when she only closed and locked the door, his smile returned.

She came closer and kissed him. Then paused and picked up a letter from his desk.

"What is this?" she asked.

"An invitation, as are the rest on that pile."

"This is to my sister's ball."

"Aye. I'm aware. I was going to ask you if you would like to attend. I know Millicent is not your favorite person, but the rest of your family might be there, and while I don't give a fig about what others think, it might seem odd that we do not attend a family function."

Lily nodded. "Yes, I'm sure you're right. I didn't think we would be so popular," she said as she flipped through the stack of invitations.

He took advantage of her inattention to sweep the few loose curls from her neck so he could put his lips against the soft skin there.

As he'd hoped, she shivered and dropped the invitations in a messy pile on the desk. Turning to him, she smiled and he swept in to kiss her greedily.

Pulling her leg up to his hip, he pushed her gown higher until a sharp knock at the door halted his progress.

"Bloody hell," Finn complained as Lily giggled and put her foot back on the floor. Going to the door, he unlocked and opened it to find the butler, Blackwood. "Yes?"

"Lord Flemming and Lord Breckenridge are here to see you, Your Grace."

"Tell them it's not a—"

"You weren't thinking to turn us away, were ye?" Shay said as he barged in with Reese on his trail.

"Good day, Your Grace," Reese said while offering a bow to Lily.

Shay wasn't satisfied with a bow and stepped close enough to take her hand and place a too-long kiss to her skin. "We missed ye when we visited yesterday, Your Grace." He practically purred her title.

With a growl, Finn moved forward and shoved his best friend away from his wife.

"That's enough of that."

Lily chuckled and shook her head, clearly amused by their antics.

"And yes, I was going to turn you away. I'm busy." Or he had been busy, trying to get under his wife's skirts. But now Lily was leaving.

She stopped and looked up at him through her dark lashes.

"I'll be upstairs resting, when you are done with your business here." She squeezed his arm before allowing her fingers to trail across his back and over his arse.

"Minx," he whispered and had every intention of following her until he heard glasses clinking.

Right. He had guests.

With another growl, he turned back to them.

"What do you want?" he snapped, unable to bank his irritation.

"By God, you were going to tup her here on your desk, weren't you? You dirty hound," Shay said with a wide grin.

"There's nothing dirty about a husband showing affection for his wife."

"Affection." Reese snorted.

Since he was closest, Finn reached out and gave him a light smack on the back of the head.

"Ouch!"

"What do you want?" Finn repeated.

Reese batted his long blond lashes that made the women swoon. Finn, not so much.

"Are you not happy to see us?"

"Not as happy as I would have been to see my wife out of her dress."

Shay held out a glass. "Sorry we've such poor timing. We only wanted to see if you were up for some fun tonight. Come to *Nuit Noire* with us."

"I was *up* for some fun a few minutes ago," Finn mumbled more to himself. To his friends he just shook his head. "I'm afraid I'm not going to be up for visiting your club, or the kind of fun you're referring to. I'm married. It's balls and musicales for me."

His friends frowned. It wasn't as if Finn spent so many nights out carousing.

"I was never good at cards before and I have no desire to spend the evening in a gaming hell. I'm a married man. A father."

"You owe me a guinea," Shay said while shoving Reese with his elbow.

With a frown aimed toward Finn, Reese pulled the coin from his waistcoat and handed it over.

"I told him you would be too caught up in your family for such runnin' about," Shay explained with his heavy brogue. The man had spent his earlier years in the Highlands and still carried the speech of his homelands. "I don't blame ye wanting to spend time with your duchess. But you should know, even your wee lad would win against the man we're playing tonight. It is a sure thing."

"Nothing is a sure thing," Finn said.

"Stevie Rockledge plays deeper when he begins to lose and doesn't know how to stop."

"Lord Percival?" Finn questioned and Reese nodded.

"Aye. You won't want to miss it."

"Watching a man bet away more than he has is not something I wish to be part of. And you shouldn't take advantage of such a sot. Don't you wish for a challenge?"

Shay let out a resigned breath and shrugged. "He's going to lose his money to someone. It may as well be me. At least I would never cheat him."

That was true enough. His friends, for as wild as they seemed, were good men.

"All the same, I plan to escort my lovely wife to a ball this evening."

Shay scrunched up his nose as if Finn had confessed to wanting to eat slugs.

"Come now, lads. Balls are not so bad once you're married. No reason to fear walking into a room alone, or turning into a dark hall. I can no longer be trapped by some sinister mama, or diabolical debutante."

Reese feigned a shiver. Nearly as tall as Shay, with blond locks the women seemed to adore, Reese was practically hunted like prey during the season.

Finn chuckled at their reaction and then sobered. "If my wife wishes to host a ball, you will both come to support her. Do you understand?"

Both men frowned before nodding and following up with an, "Aye."

"Now show us your lad."

He escorted them upstairs to the nursery and peeked inside first to make sure Lily hadn't stopped in to nurse their son before her nap. When he found only Willie in his crib, Finn put his index finger to his lips and waved them inside.

"He's a brawl lad," Shay said. "Look at the size of those mitts."

"Are we really supposed to praise ye for doing nothing but lie with a beautiful woman? No one praises me for not having any bairns. Not having them is far more difficult than having them."

Shay poked at Reese until he grumbled and said, "Ah, ye did a fine job, Finn." Under his breath, Finn heard the man say something about how it was Lily who should be praised. Finn couldn't argue there.

"Will you really not come with us this evening? The Season has already begun. There's plenty of time. Besides, you hate balls as much as we do," Reese pointed out.

"I used to hate them, but now that I have Lily on my arm, I'm actually looking forward to it."

"Do you hear this, Shay? He's gone mad. We must do something," Reese said.

Shay just shook his head slowly.

"Nay, he's not mad. He's in love."

Finn felt the word rattle through his bones and lodge in his heart. He'd wanted to find a love like his parents had. He'd always thought it would be an evasive thing. Something that would take years and dogged determination to search out. He never expected the woman of his heart to simply be waiting outside a tavern for him to stop by and pick her up. Aye, he loved her. He'd known that for some time now. But the way Shay had said it. *In love.* Seemed important in some way.

Yes, he was in love with his wife.

Maybe he hadn't noticed because it had been too easy.

He did love Lily. He loved William and he loved the life they were creating. As well as the lives he and Lily would create in the future. He wanted a large family, filled with love and laughter.

Clearing his throat, he studied the men in his study. He and his best friends had always been aligned in what they wanted from life. Freedom and happiness.

But now things had shifted. Maybe not in the goal, but in the perception of what those things meant.

"If you'll both excuse me, I must go and change so I'll be ready to escort my lovely wife to our first London event as husband and wife. I hope you both find happiness, but for me, I know it is not to be found in a gaming hell or the backrooms of the theater."

"It is still hours from you needing to prepare for the ball. We know you plan to go wake her from her nap. The poor duchess," Shay taunted.

They each patted him on the back as they left. They seemed to feel sympathy for him, while Finn felt the same for them. Interesting how one's perspective could change.

To think Finn had been like them a year ago and now, instead of seeking out darker entertainment, he was looking forward to walking into the Addington's ball with his beautiful wife on his arm. And tonight when they returned home, he planned to ravish her and tell her how he felt for her.

Chapter Thirty-Five

L ILY SHIFTED IN her seat yet again as her maid did her best to affix the pearl strands through Lily's hair. She hardly recognized herself as she stared at her reflection in the looking glass.

At two and twenty, she'd not been a young girl when she came out the year before, but she'd been incredibly naïve and desperate for affection. Now she seemed mature and settled. Perhaps even patient, except for her inability to sit still.

"There. How is that?" her maid asked.

Twisting her head this way and that, Lily was pleased with the look as well as the stability of her coiffure.

"Thank you, Belinda. It is lovely."

A brisk knock had Lily turn toward the door as it opened and her dashing husband entered with William in his arms.

"Look how beautiful your mama looks this evening, Willie," Finn said before tilting his head and frowning. "But I do think something is missing, don't you?"

"Missing?" Lily looked down at her ruby gown and silver dancing slippers.

When she looked up, she saw Finn hand William to Belinda as he came closer holding a box.

"I had my solicitor send the Granton jewels to the house

today and took the liberty of asking your maid what color you were wearing tonight. I do hope I chose correctly."

He opened the lid displaying a sparkling ruby and diamond choker and earbobs to match.

"Oh, how perfect."

Finn helped her by fastening the necklace as she handled the bobs.

"*You* are perfect, wife."

Her cheeks warmed under his compliment. She gazed at him in the reflection of the looking glass and saw deep affection in his amber eyes. It might have been due to their plans in the study being cut short, but she thought it was more than lust.

"Thank you, Finn."

"Shall we?"

She nodded and went to Belinda to press a kiss to Willie's chubby cheek.

"I'll see him up to the nursery," Belinda said as Finn blew against Willie's palm making him smile. He'd been doing that more these days and Lily was eager to hear him laugh.

Finn assisted Lily into their carriage and soon they were away to her sister's home a few streets away.

"I'm nervous," she admitted.

"I'll be by your side ready to unleash my ducal glare at anyone who isn't enraptured by your charm and beauty."

She laughed as was his intent.

"Thank you," she said more for his role in calming her nerves than his promise to glare. "It is sad to say I would be less nervous if we were attending the ball of a complete stranger rather than Millie's."

"Yes, well, it does seem as though we are willingly walking into the witch's lair. And your brothers-in-law are quite repulsive. Except, Harry."

"Harry hardly speaks."

"Yes. That's why he's not horrid."

"And my brothers?"

"I worry for them."

"Aren't young men encouraged to be scamps in their bache-lordom?"

"Scamps, yes. But I fear Max plays too deeply at the tables and doesn't know when to stop. And Matthew seems to want to follow in his footsteps. But then your father…" He shook his head. "Good God, Lily, how did you come from this family and turn out somewhat normal."

She brushed at her skirt and lifted a brow. "I'm going to ignore your use of the word, *somewhat.*"

"Thank you, dear."

Finn helped her down from the carriage when they arrived and he held her hand against his arm tightly as they walked into Millie's home, as if sending his own courage through to her by touch.

"The Duke and Duchess of Granton," the majordomo announced them and everyone in the room turned to stare.

"My, but that surely did it," Finn said.

Lily didn't answer, she was too busy taking in the crowd below them as she took the steps into the ballroom. Many a fan had come up between the women as they huddled closer together to whisper.

"I've never caused such a stir on my own. This is surely all your doing," he whispered.

She couldn't help but laugh. While some of the women were looking at her, their narrowed gazes told her they were jealous she had taken this charming man off the marriage mart.

"Your Graces," Millie said formally. "Welcome to our home."

"Thank you. I hope to have you, Martha, and Maribel for tea soon."

"Of course." Millie's lips pinched together, making her look more like their eldest sister. "Mother is also in town."

"Oh. I hadn't heard. I will be sure to invite her as well."

"I hope you enjoy your time here this evening," Millie said as a way to get them moving along.

"That wasn't so bad," Finn said.

"No. She didn't even sneer. I'm not sure what to think of it."

"Do not let down your guard. That's when you are most vulnerable to their spells."

Lily laughed again.

"Will you be going off to find the gaming rooms?" she asked, earning a confused look from Finn.

"No. I said I would be by your side this evening. I'm not about to leave you here alone with all these scoundrels eyeing you up. I daresay, I will need to step out into the garden to find a large stick so as to fend them away from my wife."

She laughed again. She would need to find a way to thank her husband later for helping her through this event. His humor had managed to calm her brittle nerves.

After dancing the first set with her husband, she was asked to dance by two other gentlemen. Though they hadn't asked her as much as they'd asked Finn who nodded his permission. She danced a waltz with Finn and then another set with him before Lord Neville came to ask for her to stand with him.

She'd never danced so much at one ball. It was strange how easy it was to converse with men when the stress of marriage was removed.

"That's the woman who trapped the Duke of Granton." Lily heard a woman say as she leaned in to her friend. Lily stumbled, but continued on. As she made her way to the dance floor with Lord Neville, she heard other whispers…

"Who *is* she? I've never seen her before."

"She's quite old, isn't she?"

"That's why she was so desperate as to capture him."

"My sister set quite a trap indeed." That last voice was Millie's. Lily shouldn't have been surprised to find her own sister speaking of her in such a way. And in reality, she had no defense. She hadn't tried to trap Finn, but she had nonetheless.

As the dance continued, the whispers grew louder, until they seemed to swirl around her in an icy fog. Just as Finn had warned, she shouldn't have let her guard down for a moment.

For the evil spells had been cast.

Chapter Thirty-Six

F INN'S GAZE SEARCHED his wife's face when she returned to his side.

"You look rather pale. Did Lord Neville say something untoward?"

Lily looked up at him with those wide gray eyes and shook her head. "He was polite enough."

"Then what is the matter?" he asked more firmly, because it was clear something was wrong.

"I'm well. I just need to go to the retiring room. I'll be back shortly."

Before he could offer to escort her, she spun and hurried away from him to disappear in the crush of people.

He waited for a few moments and then a while longer before giving up and making his way toward the exit leading to the corridor. He didn't know where the lady's retiring room was, but assumed it would be down this hall.

He wanted to get out of the stifling room, but more importantly, he wanted to speak to Lily quietly. If someone had said something to upset her, they would leave that instant.

He'd been proud to enter the room with such a beautiful woman on his arm, but he'd heard a few whispers insinuating Lily had trapped him into marriage. He wasn't sure how such a rumor had been started, but didn't put it past a harpy such as Millicent.

Finn leaned against the wall, waiting for Lily. He wouldn't be sorry to leave now. He wished to know who had come up with the rule that couples should dance no more than three times at an event. And why would such a rule apply to husbands and wives? No doubt most men of the ton leaned on such a rule to get out of having to touch their wives.

Finn was so intent on watching for Lily, he didn't realize someone had come to stand close to him.

Finn turned to look at the man with a questioning raise of his brows. He didn't know this person. Or at least he didn't think they had ever met. He'd seen him at his old haunts with Reese and Shay. Finn recalled he was a loud, obnoxious man.

On appearances alone, Finn didn't think he wanted to make acquaintances with the gentleman. He had a snide smile on his lips and an unsavory glint in his blue eyes.

"Might I have a word alone, Your Grace?"

Letting out a sigh, Finn gave a nod and followed the man to a different corridor.

"What can I do for you, Lord...?"

"Mister. Mister Reginald Flockton."

Finn said nothing else, just waited for the man to get on with it. No doubt he wanted money for some flighty investment scheme or wanted Finn to fund an invention. Finn was not expecting his next words.

"It is beyond intriguing how the son of the third son of a baron will one day be a duke, is it not?"

Finn schooled his reaction, though it was clear this man was the weasel-arse that had abandoned Lily.

"I'm afraid I don't know what you mean."

The man's eyes went wide in feigned surprise.

"Please tell me she didn't try to pass my child off as yours. Unless..." the man leaned closer and Finn caught a burning whiff of gin on his breath. "Did she take you to her bed that same day?

Then I guess it could be yours. I thought she would have needed a few days to get over me, at least."

Finn looked about the hall and when he found they were alone, he grabbed the man by his cravat and shoved him against the wall.

"I'll ask you to watch what you say about my wife."

The man didn't even wince at being held by his neck. Finn imagined such a man was probably threatened on a daily basis. What had Lily seen in this scoundrel?

But, of course, he knew the answer. She'd seen an escape from her life of being ignored and forgotten. This blighter had pretended to care for her, made her feel as if she were special. And then left her.

The man chuckled and Finn let him slither down the wall to his feet. It would be better if they didn't look suspicious if someone were to find them in the hall. And he didn't want Lily to come out to see them fighting. Finn was better than this.

"Don't worry. I'm not going to say anything. As long as you give me a reason not to."

Finn glared at the man as his words fell into place.

The weasel of an arse was attempting to blackmail him.

"I'm sure there are plenty of people in the House of Lords who would want to know the Earl of Haliday is not the rightful heir of the dukedom."

Finn laughed. The whole situation was preposterous.

"Lily and I were married when he was born. He is my son. No one will question a duke."

"Will they question a duchess?" he asked. "If you're not worried about my boy losing his title, then maybe you care about your wife's reputation."

Again, he was reaching. Right or wrong, when he married Lily she and their child were marked beyond reproach. However, he'd heard the gossip that Lily had trapped him. He didn't believe it for a moment but those rumors along with Mr. Flockton's allegations could be damning.

Finn knew better than to let the man see any hint of doubt.

"You think the ton will believe the word of you, the third son of a baron, over a duke?"

"I don't need anyone to believe me. I only need them to doubt her."

Finn had reached the end of his patience.

"You won't have the option to cast doubts when you're lying face up in Hyde Park with my bullet in your gut. I shall see you at dawn along with your second. I demand satisfaction."

The man turned pale and his lips fell from the smug smile into a gaping hole.

"Bu-but I was not going to ask for such a large sum." Shaking his head, he changed tack once more. "I was only jesting."

"So, you did not leave a woman in a tavern in Scotland with no funds after you'd ruined her?"

"Well… she knew it was just for the night. I never made any promises."

"But you did. You promised to marry her."

"She's lying." He must have realized that was the wrong thing to say for he shook his head and tried yet again to talk himself out of certain death. "That is, yes. I might have made it sound like I planned to marry her, but she left willingly."

"Dawn. If you are not there, I will hunt you down like the cowardly slug you are. Now get out of my sight before I choke the life from you here in my evening clothes."

The man didn't need a second warning. He scurried off like the weasel Lily had named him. Finn wondered if the man would even show up for the duel. If he had enough honor to do so, Finn would see the monster never preyed on another naïve young lady ever again.

It was hard to ruin someone from the grave.

A door farther down the hall opened and Beatrice came forward laughing with another young woman.

"That should teach her for taking the man that was supposed to be mi—" She froze when she saw him standing there and her cat's grin pulled up her lips. "Good evening, Your Grace. I was hoping you would seek me out for a dance this evening."

"I am waiting for my wife. I assume she is in the retiring room?" Was he the person Beatrice was just speaking about? Was he the one she thought was supposed to be hers? Had she done something to Lily?

Finn was still too angry to deal with the wench

"I didn't see her in there, did you, Miss Stife?"

"Well… uh…" Looking between an enraged duke and Beatrice, the woman seemed to weigh her options. "Yes, she is inside. She seemed… upset."

Beatrice huffed and smiled up at him.

"Should we dance?" she said as if she hadn't noticed the fire in his eyes. Then she placed her hands on his arm. "I know you didn't want her. She trapped you. It is only fair you should be allowed to do what you want."

"Get out of my sight."

Beatrice looked surprised, but must have finally noticed he was livid. She and Miss Stife hurried away. Finn stormed toward the retiring room just as Lily came out, her gown wet and her eyes red.

His anger doubled as he went to her.

"What happened?"

"'Tis nothing. I was careless with the water is all."

She was lying to him.

She probably thought brushing off whatever Beatrice had done was the easiest course. Or mayhap she didn't think to bother him. She was always trying not to be a bother for anyone.

"We are leaving," he said, trying to hold in his fury with her, with Beatrice, with Flockton, with everyone it seemed.

Lily followed along behind him in silence as they went to their carriage and he told the driver to take them home immediately.

"It is not so bad. It's only a bit of water," she said, unknowing to everything else that had transpired that evening

"Reginald Flockton, Lily?" he said while rubbing his temples where a headache had started.

Lily gasped and he didn't need to look at her to see her large eyes were wide in shock.

"You couldn't see what a rotter he was? I only knew the man for a few seconds and could see the filth oozing from him."

"What did he say?" she asked.

"Why? If I tell you he didn't say anything about being the man you fled to Scotland to marry, would you lie to me as you did about what Beatrice did to your gown this evening?"

"I—I meant only to—"

"Not be a bother?" he finished for her. It seemed he was angry at her, though he wasn't sure why. She was the one who'd been wronged. Still, he couldn't help himself. "The situation has become quite a bother when he attempted to blackmail me to keep his silence about your son's parentage."

Lily gasped again and he knew why. He'd never referred to William as her son. It was always *their* son. Ever since the moment they'd wed. But it slipped out now at the worst possible time.

"If it is the money, you can use the funds from my dowry to pay him."

"Pay him? Don't you understand anything, Lily? That's not how it works. If we pay him today, he'll just come back tomorrow and the day after that and the day after that."

They had arrived home and he allowed the footman to hand her down. He couldn't touch her at the moment, not when he was so furious. Not that he was in any danger of causing her harm, but to touch her would surely dissolve his frustrations and he wasn't ready to let go of his anger.

As they entered the house she headed for the stairs, but he stopped her.

"Leave us," he said to the servants in the foyer. When they were alone, he said, "I will take care of this as men take care of things. It is the only way."

"A duel? You cannot shoot him, Finn."

"I can. Isn't that what I do? Take care of your *unfortunate situations?*"

She flinched away from him as if he'd hit her. He understood he was being beastly to the person who had been wronged by everyone, and now apparently him as well. But his temper had been ignited and words came out he didn't mean.

Rubbing his temples again, he shook his head. "Forgive me, Lily. I didn't mean that. I have much to do to defend your honor."

"I don't need you to defend me. Who cares if he tells everyone? You told me it didn't matter, that we were above it."

"You think I'm to sit back as that snake disparages my wife's name? If you don't care for yourself, think of William and what this will mean for him. A cloud of doubt over him all his life. Is that what you want?"

"Of course not, but Reggie is no one against the word of a duke."

"He *is* someone, Lily. You made him someone when you ran off with him. When you loved him."

"This is not about me or my honor, or even about William. This is about your pride. Don't you see, Finn? This is what he does."

"It is too late now. It is done. If you'll excuse me." He went to his study and penned two notes and sent footmen out to find Reese and Shay. Chances were good they would be together, but having two messages meant they'd be found quicker.

Going to his desk, he pulled out the wooden box that had been there as long as he could remember. He opened it to see the dueling pistols that once belonged to his father.

As far as Finn knew, his father had never had need of them. Finn was surprised to be needing them himself. Despite his Scot's blood, he was normally slow to anger. But he had reached his limit when Reginald Flockton had threatened his family.

He poured a second glass of whisky when the first one was

gone. He was on his fourth when Reese and Shay were announced by the butler.

"What's happened?" Shay asked.

Finn threw back the remains of his glass and wiped his mouth with the sleeve of his coat.

"I need one of you to be my second. You can decide who gets the honor."

"Bloody hell," Reese said.

Bloody hell, indeed.

Chapter Thirty-Seven

LILY HOVERED AT the top of the stairs, unsure of what to do.
Finn would be leaving for a duel in a few hours and she
needed to find some way to stop him.

She didn't know much about dueling, but to know it was the
way honorable men handled a perceived slight. But Reggie was
not honorable.

The door to the study opened and Finn's friends came out,
muttering to themselves.

"The duchess is a lovely woman, don't get me wrong, but no
woman is worth this kind of trouble. No matter how beautiful."

Shay was right. She wasn't worth this risk.

"Are you going to call it off?" she asked, hurrying down the
steps to intercept them. "Were you able to talk him out of this?"

"Nay. There's no talking Finn out of something he'd decided
to do."

"Stubborn Scot. What if he is killed?" she fretted.

"You'll be fine enough, being the mother of his heir."

Lily tilted her head to the side. Did they not know the truth?

"He didn't tell you the reason for the duel?"

"Nay," Shay said, almost seeming surprised she would ask.
"He called on us and we'll stand by him. We don't need to know
the reason."

Reese leaned a bit closer to her to whisper, "I do wonder. Did he catch the two of you—"

"Of course not! I would never be unfaithful to my husband."

"I told ye, dunderhead. She's not that way. And Finn would have had the man strung up by his balls without the formality of a duel."

"Very well. I can't say I'm not curious as to what would bring Finn to this step. He's generally reasonable. But we must be off, we need to find a surgeon."

"A surgeon?" Lily felt faint and sat on the step so she wouldn't fall over.

"What is wrong with ye, Reese? You don't say such a thing to a lady."

"Sorry, Your Grace. I'm sure he'll be fine. He's a good shot."

Lily thought of something she needed them to know. If this was going to happen, she wanted them armed with as much knowledge as possible.

"He might try to cheat."

Both sets of eyes came back to her looking confused.

"Mr. Flockton, not Finn. The man is a liar and a cheat. Watch him closely."

"Aye. We will," Shay promised.

"And gentlemen?" she said, her voice failing her as tears welled and streamed down her cheeks. "Please make sure my husband comes home."

They'd made their empty promises before leaving for their gruesome task of finding a surgeon. Still, she couldn't just sit there hoping for the best.

Going to the duchess' chambers she'd yet to sleep in, she went to the escritoire and penned a note, allowing the words to flow from her heart through her pen.

She left it on the table next to the bed where she and Finn had planned to spend the night wrapped in each other's arms.

She could not bear to just sit there waiting to hear word of the outcome of the duel. If Finn was killed, she would not withstand the weight of that guilt on top of all the rest. She would surely be crushed.

Finn had taken this on because of her. He'd taken on so much more because of her. She'd been a fool to think he would not one day resent her for it. Well, that day seemed to be tonight. She would no longer be something he must fix. She wouldn't be his burden.

Rushing up to the nursery, she and Sara bundled up a sleeping William and went down the back stairs and out to the stables to find the coachman. Soon enough they were on their way to the one place she'd never felt welcome but hoped she would this night.

The butler opened the door on her knock and frowned.

"Please. I know it is late, but I must see my sister. It cannot wait. Please tell Martha I am here."

FINN'S ANGER HAD fled somewhere between the fifth glass of whisky and Shay taking the bottle away.

"You'll need to be able to stand if you plan on dueling," the large man said.

"Not to mention his wits," Reese added in.

"Nay, wits are nay needed for dueling," Shay argued. "Wits just get in the way of it."

Finn wanted to ask him how many duels he'd been in, but if it were even one it would be more than Finn. What had he done?

Mayhap the more important question would be why had he done it?

It was easy enough to say it had been to protect Lily's reputation. To protect William from gossip. But Lily had been right. It had been his pride. Seeing that arrogant arse call William his son and knowing it was true had brought Finn's blood to boiling.

Finn was William's father. Finn was Lily's husband. And that weasel planned to ruin everything they'd built together. A family. His family.

"Go and change."

"Does it matter what I'm wearing?" Finn looked down at himself. "If I end up dead I'll already be in my finest."

"You'll not end up dead if you go change into something that allows more motion than these bindings. Can ye even get out of that coat without your valet?"

Only if he wanted to ruin it in the process.

With a sigh, he stood and headed for the door.

"Shirtsleeves and a waistcoat would be best," Shay ordered as Finn took the stairs. In his room, Finn noticed the note before he'd the chance to call Thomas to help him change.

He opened it slowly almost expecting what the words would say. He wasn't wrong.

Finn,

I'm beyond sorry for everything. It seems my ill luck has spread even to those who were trying to help me. I never wanted to be a burden. I never wanted you to resent William and I for our pasts. I'm sorry it has come to that. And worse that you would put yourself in danger for us. I cannot bear it, to see you hurt or worse because of us.

William and I have gone. You can petition for divorce, and move on with your life without us darkening your name or the title.

I knew it was selfish to take your offer of marriage. But being with you was more than I could resist. Even so, I will not see a good man hurt for my selfish recklessness.

I know you think I married you because I had no other options. And it is true my options were quite limited. But it's important that you know my situation is not the only reason I agreed to marry you. I would have said yes even if my future had not looked so grim. Obviously, William was the reason you asked, but he was not the reason I said yes. I agreed simply because I wanted to be with you. I will always cherish the time I spent with you.

Please call off the duel. I will take care of my own messes from here.

Forever grateful,
Lily

"Forever grateful?" Finn nearly choked. He'd never wanted her to be grateful. He'd only done what was right. Except he wasn't sure that was true.

He'd been selfish as well. He'd found a woman who made him smile and laugh when both of those things had been beyond him for more than a year. She'd made him happy and he'd stepped up because he'd wanted to be with her.

He'd claimed her not because she was without options but because he'd wanted her. And then he'd allowed his anger to poison everything between them.

He went to the room next to theirs and found it empty. The jewels he'd given her were sitting on the dressing table.

Leaving the room, he considered going upstairs to the nursery, but knew finding it empty would crush him. Instead, he went down to the study where his friends were pacing.

"I thought you were going to change," Shay complained.

"I don't need to change. I'm going to fire wide, Flockton will see that and fire wide himself and it will be over."

"A moment ago, you wanted him dead? Not that you told us what information he planned to use to blackmail you."

"A moment ago, I hadn't read the note Lily wrote telling me she left me and expects me to seek a divorce."

They both gasped in shock. Reese was the one to say, "Why?"

He'd not planned to tell them. He wanted the secret to die with Flockton. But with no permanent ending to the duel, he didn't know what the weasel would do. If Lily was strong enough to bear the rumors, Finn would not fail her. He would be strong as well.

But he would rather his friends knew the truth rather than

hear it from others.

"William is not my blood. He is Flockton's. But he is my son in every way."

"Did Lily trick you into thinking he was yours?" Reese asked. Handsome and rich as Reese was, he was the constant target of title-hunting ladies. It was not a surprise he would think such a thing.

"Ye are going to end up on the dueling field for saying such," Shay said. "Of course, she didn't trick him. She's not that way. Ye saw the way she looked at Finn. She's in love with him."

"Of course," Reese said quickly. "My apologies."

"She didn't trick me. Flockton left her after promising marriage. I found her sitting on the steps of a tavern with more than a dozen drunkards planning to make things worse for her. I brought her with me to save her, but in truth she saved me. And then we learned she was with child and it gave me a reason to offer for her. But William is my son in every way but one, is that clear?"

"You'll never hear any different from us. And we'll stand by ye when you call Flockton a liar."

"I'm sure he is on his way to America as we speak. But if not, let's go and make sure he knows the three of us plan to denounce his claims. He'll be made a fool and it should keep his tongue still enough," Reese said while straightening his coat.

Finn really did have the best friends. And the best family.

"And when this is over you can go find your lass and set things right with her."

"She thinks she's a burden. And I didn't do anything to dispel her of such a thing. I was angry and said things…"

"Then you will say better things. Say the most important thing to get her back."

Finn nodded and handed the case of pistols to Shay who had the poor luck of being Finn's second. At least, there would be no blood spilled this day.

Chapter Thirty-Eight

L ILY HELD HER sleeping baby as she watched the coming sun turn the sky a hazy pink. It was almost dawn.

She didn't know what would happen. Had Finn found her letter? Had he called off the foolish duel? If not, would someone be hurt this day? Would someone die?

While she'd once hated Reggie with every part of her being for what he'd done, her anger had resolved into disinterest. He wasn't worth any passion even hatred. He was no one.

He could not hurt her any longer for he didn't hold even a sliver of her heart.

But Finn...

A soft knock came, followed by Martha's presence.

"I figured you would be awake," she said softly as she came closer and brushed a hand over William's downy blond hair.

It had only been a few hours since Martha had been pulled from her bed to find Lily pacing in her drawing room in tears.

Lily told her sister everything, from thinking she'd fallen in love with Reggie to realizing she was in love with Finn. So in love, she was willing to walk away if it meant he would be safe.

"I'm worried he might still go through with it."

Martha waved her hand. "Men do many foolish things, but most don't cause lasting harm. I'm sure he will be knocking upon my door and begging you to come home soon enough."

That was what their father would have done for Mama, because it was what was expected. Their mother wouldn't come home for anything less than a full round of begging. But Lily was not like their mother. She didn't want Finn to beg her to stay. He had already done enough for her. And now she needed to do what was right for him.

"Thank you for allowing us to stay with you last night," Lily said to change the subject.

Martha shook her head.

"We are sisters. Perhaps not as close as we should be, but I think the two of us could be friends. You are welcome to stay."

While Martha hadn't said how long they were welcome to stay, Lily knew there would be a limit. It was true, she and Martha had become closer, Lily wasn't certain what might happen when Finn filed for divorce. Lily would be tainted with scandal. And Martha would not want Lily's shame as a shadow over her home.

Lily would need to find another way.

But this time she was not without funds. She had her dowry which Finn had put aside for her. And unlike the last time when she'd faced the unknown, she was no longer a naïve girl.

Her dowry would be enough to keep her and William comfortable if she planned wisely. She only needed to decide where to go, and no one would ever find her again.

$$\text{Chapter Thirty-Nine}$$

FINN FROWNED AT the man standing opposite him. Flockton must not have had friends to stop him from drinking last night or to take on the duty of being a second. For all his apparent charm, he was without any real companionship.

How silly Finn had been a year ago when he'd felt so alone. He hadn't been as alone as this man.

"When this is over, Flockton, there will be no more talk of blackmail. You'll speak to no one of Lily or my son. Do you understand?"

He nodded, more a bob of agreement.

Both men were instructed to choose their weapons. Finn allowed Flockton to pick first as Finn knew neither pistol had been tampered with.

Turning his back on Flockton, Reese announced that each would step off ten paces and then turn and fire.

Finn had decided to aim skyward so Flockton would see there was no danger. He could only hope Flockton followed his plan and the two could leave with honor intact.

But it was as Reese called out the number eight that someone gasped, another yelled, "Watch out."

However, it was too late. Flockton had fired and shot Finn in the back. Finn was most put out by this fact as he dropped to the ground on his stomach, his unfired pistol still in his hand.

"Finn!" Reese called, and he and Shay crowded around him.

"Bloody hell, the blighter cheated," Shay said as if appalled by the man's cowardice more so than the fact Finn had been shot.

Finn was forced to acknowledge that a man could die from a coward's bullet as easily as from a man of honor. It almost seemed silly. Well, not almost. It was outright ridiculous.

If he died because of Reginald Flockton, he would miss out on watching Willie grow into a man. He would never have more children with Lily. He would never have the chance to touch his wife, or tell her he loved her.

That, at least, could be remedied.

"Reese," Finn panted as he tried not to move because moving hurt like blazes.

"Yes. I'm here, Finn."

"Tell Lily I love her. Take care of them."

"Take care of your family yourself. And we're not about to be delivering messages for stubborn dukes," Shay said. Which was why he'd asked Reese to deliver the message.

He hoped his more reasonable friend would tell her. For if the fiery pain in his back was any indication, he feared he might not have the chance.

LILY AND MARTHA were coming down for breakfast when there was an insistent knock at the door.

"What did I say?" Martha gloated with a warm smile. "Although it is too early for him to have bought flowers. Pity."

The butler opened the door and Lily realized she had been hoping Finn had come for her only when it was Reese who entered and asked for her.

"Please I must speak to the Duchess of Granton. Is she here?"

Before the butler could answer, Lily did.

"I'm here, Reese," she said even though she wanted to run far and fast from whatever news he brought.

"It is Finn. He's been shot. Please. You must come home. You and William."

All plans of running away were somehow forgotten when Reese looked at her with fear in his brown eyes.

She could not hide away here at Martha's. Not when Finn needed her.

The house was in chaos when she entered the foyer. Sending Sara up to the nursery with William, Lily turned to take matters into hand.

"Where is the duke?" she asked the most important question.

"He's in here. We didn't want to risk moving him up the stairs so we put him in the parlor," Shay said at her side. Lily entered to see the furniture had been pushed aside except for the chaise where her husband lay on his stomach, his face turned toward her.

She took in his pale skin and instead of crumbling into hysterics as she would have liked, she jumped into action.

"Where's the surgeon?"

"Over there," he pointed to a young man by the windows, opening the drapes. He was most likely assessing the best light with which to see to save her husband.

Lily nodded and called for the housekeeper to bring shears. They would need to cut away Finn's clothing.

"Please tell the kitchen to bring hot water and linens." Turning to the man who couldn't be much older than she, she asked, "Do you need anything else, Doctor?"

"A table, right here." He pointed to the place where the floor was bright with the morning sun.

Lily found two footmen to bring in a table from the library that would be sturdy enough to hold Finn while the man worked.

Soon enough they were moving Finn to the table.

Lily bent close to his head and stroked his light brown hair back from his damp face.

"I am here, love. I shouldn't have left you. I am here," she promised. She placed a kiss to his temple and turned to the doctor. "Please save my husband," Lily begged.

"I will do my best, Your Grace."

It was most difficult for Lily to turn and leave him there.

In the hall, she found Reese and Shay muttering to themselves.

"What happened?"

"Flockton shot him on eight paces instead of waiting until ten. Finn was planning to shoot wide. Had the coward seen that, he would have done the same and all would have been over without bloodshed, but he cheated."

"I am not surprised," Lily said. "He is a liar and a debaucher of innocents, why would cheating not be expected of such a weasel?"

"I do think you are maligning weasels by referring to him as one."

"You're right," she agreed with Reese. "If his bullet ends my husband, he will be swinging from a rope." Lily had not realized she was capable of such viciousness, but this was Finn and he had been hurt by the man who had betrayed her.

"That might be difficult, Your Grace. He's run for America. His older brother said he put him on a ship. He was tired of the pup causing so much trouble and this was the last straw. You'll never have to worry about seeing him again."

"Good. I only wish Harold would have grown weary of Reggie *before* he shot my husband." She paced in a tight circle. She knew she was expected to remain calm, for racing about the corridor was unladylike, especially for a duchess, but movement helped, for whatever reason.

"He told me to tell you he loved you," Reese said quietly. "You and William."

Shay smacked the man in the arm. "Ye were only supposed to tell her if he wasna able to. He'll be awake soon enough and he'll be able to tell her himself."

"He didn't say anything about the timing."

"Only because he didn't have the chance before he lost consciousness. He was only worried he might not wake up. But he will. His injury is not so bad. I've seen worse."

Finn had told Lily how Shay was raised in the shady parts of Inverness as a boy and only found out he was the heir to a marquisate when he was eleven. She imagined Shay had seen plenty in those early years on the street.

She hated to think of a young boy being raised so roughly, but his experiences were helpful now for putting her mind at ease.

As were Reese's words that Finn loved her. But hearing the words did not surprise her. Even for not having heard them from Finn before. Somehow, she already knew. Everything he'd done for them was proof of his affections.

He might have brushed it off as a gentleman's actions or doing the proper thing, but she saw the way he'd looked at her when they made love and she'd seen the way his eyes lit up when William reached for Finn that first time.

He was a man who loved them.

And she'd walked away when he'd needed her.

"I thought I was doing the right thing," she fretted.

"Pardon, Your Grace?" Reese said.

She shook her head. "Nothing. I need to speak to him. I need to tell him how sorry I am for leaving him like I did. I was afraid I would bring shame on his name and title."

Shay shook his head. "He'd face a wagon full of shame with his head held high for the two of ye."

Lily forced a smile and nodded. "He will wake up so I can tell him?"

"Aye, lass. He'll wake up."

Lily grasped onto Shay's promise with both hands.

Eventually the surgeon came out looking a bit tired if not hopeful. He oversaw the moving of Finn to his bed so he'd be more comfortable.

"I was able to get the ball out. It didn't hit any organs, but he's lost a fair amount of blood. Give him beef broth to build up his energy, and laudanum for the pain. I'll return later this evening."

"Thank you, Doctor."

With a nod, the man was gone and Lily was in the bed chamber she'd slept in with Finn since they'd arrived. With the exception of last night.

Reese and Shay took turns sitting with her until night came and she chased them off to their beds. The surgeon had returned and said Finn was not running a fever and that it was a good sign.

Lily had Sara bring William to her so she could hold her son for a while.

"I think he has grown in the few hours since I've seen him last," she said as she stroked a finger down her son's dimpled hand. His golden lashes lay across his cheek.

She looked at the man sleeping in the bed.

"I'm here, Finn. We're both here. Please wake up."

― ❧ ―

Chapter Forty

FINN FELT AS if he was oversleeping and missing something important. The last he'd felt this way was when he was attending Cambridge and missed an exam. But this felt more important, and no matter how much he tried he couldn't get himself to move and wake up.

Then he heard a voice that settled his nerves.

"I'm here, Finn." It was Lily.

Now he wanted to wake all the more so he could see her. He needed to tell her something. It took another moment or two to remember what it was.

He was sorry.

He'd acted like a brute when they'd left her sister's ball. He'd been angry and had taken it out on her. Which made no sense because he loved her.

Oh, yes. That was the other thing he needed to tell her.

Pushing against the heavy weight, his lids flickered open into the dimness. It had been dawn when he'd gone to duel with Flockton, but now it seemed to be night. His eyes focused on Lily and their son, who was asleep in her arms.

She was singing softly, her voice in perfect tune.

He smiled and listened. When the melody cut off and he heard her sniffle, he realized she was crying. He couldn't allow her to worry.

"Lily," he managed in a dry, croaking voice.

Her head shot up and her gray, watery eyes went wide.

"Finn," she came closer, her abrupt standing earned a grumble from their son as she shifted him. "I'm here," she said as she'd been telling him occasionally while he'd slept.

He'd heard her before and wanted to reach out to her, but couldn't until now.

She took his hand and he noticed how warm it was when usually her hands were cooler than his. She looked at the baby and then to the pitcher by the bed.

She settled Willie on the bed next to him and Finn was able to pat the lad on the back softly while Lily brought Finn a glass of water.

She held it to his lips and he drank. He might have argued, but even a few pats had tired him and he wasn't certain he could manage the full glass.

"Thank you," he said, before recalling the reason he'd forced himself awake. "Lily, I'm sorry. You were right. It was pride that made me go to the park."

"Shh… You don't need to apologize. I'm sorry, I left when I should have stayed."

"I didn't mean what I said. Any of it. I was so frustrated that I couldn't protect you and Willie properly. I was angry with myself, not you."

"All is forgiven."

"I love you, Lily. And I love William. You are my family. I never want you to leave. Whatever happens, we will face it together."

She nodded and leaned closer to press a kiss to his head.

"And I never want *you* to leave *us*."

"Never," he whispered before falling asleep.

They left London as soon as Finn was healed enough for travel. He'd been able to vote for Shay's bill so his responsibilities in London were completed.

Lily had said her goodbyes to Martha and her brothers, but she was excited to go home to *Gealach* Castle.

William reached for Finn as they walked to the carriage.

"I can have Sara take him for a while."

"Nay. I'll take him."

Lily worried their heavy son would be too much for her healing husband to carry, but he wouldn't hear of it. The baby smiled at him, and when Finn leaned down to blow against his neck, William laughed.

Finn and Lily shared a look of surprise before Finn did it again, getting the same reaction from their son.

Throughout their trip north, they both tried different things to make Willie laugh. It was an entertaining distraction.

Lily was nearly starved when they pulled up to a tavern. Finn helped her down from the carriage with a smirk. It wasn't until she was on the ground and looked up at the sign that she realized where they were. The Old Forge Inn.

She recognized those steps all too well from spending hours sitting on them waiting for someone to come along and help her. She never would have guessed the man who had finally offered his aid would also offer his name as well as his heart.

"I seem to remember the place served a tasty mutton pie."

Lily passed Willie off to Sara so she could go in for dinner with her husband.

"What if someone recognizes me?" Lily said.

Finn merely shrugged off any concern. "We will face it together as we will face anything to come."

She nodded and they went inside to a private dining room. No one questioned the duke and duchess as they ate.

When they stepped out, Finn held out his hand to assist her down the stairs.

"I thought my life was over," she said, looking at the place she'd sat for those troubling hours baking under the sun. "But it was only the beginning."

Finn leaned down and kissed her right there in front of the

tavern full of rowdy Scots.

"Thank you for waiting for me to get here," he said.

"Always."

Epilogue

Three years later, Scotland

FINN SQUEEZED HIS son's hand as they stepped up to the familiar stone. Willie had wanted to carry the flowers. He was headstrong like his mother, something that would do him well later in life, if not for a three-year old.

"Here, Papa?" he asked, pointing to the stone.

"Aye. They are for Auntie June."

Willie's blond brows pulled together before he pointed. "Junie."

Finn turned to see Lily carrying their daughter, Juniper.

"This is your sister, June," Finn explained while taking his daughter who would be two in May. She instantly squirmed to be put down. "This was my sister, June. She was my very best friend. Just as I'm sure Junie will be for you."

Willie ran off to climb on the lower stone of one of the ancestors he'd never met.

"I'm certain they will be best friends at some point, but now he only thinks she's loud and takes his toys while he's trying to play with them," Lily said.

"I remember my sister doing the same." He kissed his daughter who had not given up on getting down to go play with her brother.

"I don't know if I ever told you, but that night when I passed you on the steps, I thought I heard her voice telling me to help you."

She tilted her head before shaking it. "No. You never told me. I didn't realize I had her to thank."

He chuckled. "Since I don't believe in specters, I knew it was my own conscience, seeing that I did the right thing."

"I know how much you dislike it when I thank you, but I am thankful for your noble conscience. Things could have been so different for me and Willie if you hadn't stopped."

"Do you know why I dislike it when you thank me?" He finally gave up and put June down to toddle off with Willie.

Lily shook her head.

"Because I don't need to be thanked for doing the thing that led to a life of happiness. I had been just as lost and alone as you were."

"You're saying we saved each other?" She tilted her head.

After taking a glance to see the children were safe, he leaned in and kissed her with all the promise for their happy future. He rested his hand on her stomach where their third child grew.

"Aye, lass. You have given me the greatest gift of all. A family."

ABOUT THE AUTHOR

One very early morning, Allison B. Hanson woke up with a conversation going on in her head. It wasn't so much a dream as being forced awake by her imagination. Unable to go back to sleep, she gave in, went to the computer, and began writing. Years later it still hasn't stopped.

Allison lives near Hershey, Pennsylvania and writes Highlander Historical and Scottish Regencies.

Catch up with Allison on any of her social media platforms here:

Website:
allisonbhanson.wordpress.com

Facebook:
facebook.com/BlueRidgeRomance

Twitter:
@AllisonBHanson

Instagram:
@allisonbhanson

Goodreads:
goodreads.com/author/show/9860589

BookBub:
bookbub.com/authors/allison-b-hanson